HEARTWARMING

Her Summer Crush

—

Linda Hope Lee

HARLEQUIN® HEARTWARMING™

Recycling programs
for this product may
not exist in your area.

ISBN-13: 978-0-373-36782-5

Her Summer Crush

Copyright © 2016 by Linda Hope Lee

HARLEQUIN®
™ www.Harlequin.com

Printed in U.S.A.

Linda Hope Lee lives in the Pacific Northwest. She likes traveling to new places, especially to small towns that might serve as settings for her novels. In addition to contemporary romance, she writes in the romantic suspense and mystery genres. When she is not writing, she's busy creating watercolor paintings or drawing in colored pencil or pen and ink. Another pastime is photography, which she uses as inspiration for her art and for her stories. She also collects children's books and anything to do with wirehaired fox terriers.

Books by Linda Hope Lee

Harlequin Heartwarming

Eva's Deadline

Visit the Author Profile page
at Harlequin.com for more titles.

To Pearl, the new kid on the block

Acknowledgments

Many thanks to Harlequin Heartwarming
senior editor Victoria Curran and
assistant editor Dana Grimaldi for helping
to shape *Her Summer Crush*. Their expertise is
invaluable and much appreciated.

CHAPTER ONE

"CODY JARVIS! What's *he* doing here?" Luci Monroe stared at the man who'd just stepped out the back door of her parents' home. "I didn't see his name on the guest list," she added.

Her sister, Francine, set a plate of crab cakes on the buffet table. "Maybe Don invited him," she said. "Didn't he say he had a surprise for you tonight?"

"He did, but I thought he meant the combo." Luci nodded toward the musicians her older brother had hired. Their music provided a pleasant backdrop to the party celebrating Luci's graduation from Seattle's University of Washington and her return to Willow Beach.

"Cody's spotted you," Francine said. "Better put a smile on your face."

"I'll be okay. I've been over him for at least

a year." And yet, as she watched him approach, her heart was beating wildly.

"C'mere, Luci." Cody opened his arms and swept her up in a warm embrace.

With a resigned sigh, she looped her arms around his neck and hugged him back.

He drew away and let his gaze rove over her. "Lookin' good, Luci."

"Thanks. You, too."

And he did. She always thought the cliché "tall, dark and handsome" suited him perfectly, and that still held true. He'd let his hair grow a little longer, but she liked it that way. And his brown-eyed gaze was as sharp as ever.

Cody hugged Francine. "Hey, Fran, good to see you."

"Hello, Cody." Francine returned his hug.

Don joined them, carrying two bottles of beer. He handed one to Cody. "Here you go, buddy. Glad you could make it." He turned to Luci. "How do you like your surprise?"

Luci propped her hands on her hips. "He's a surprise, all right. I thought he was in Timbuktu or some other exotic place."

Cody tossed his head back and laughed.

"I'll have to put that on my list. No, I just got back from Italy."

"Still the freelance photographer?" Luci said, although she didn't know why she asked when she knew the answer.

"Always." Cody patted the camera attached to a leather strap slung around his neck. "And here you are, all graduated and degreed and starting a new job, I hear."

The mention of her job brought a smile to Luci's lips. "Right. I'm working for Glen Thomas at the chamber of commerce. Writing, of course. Articles, brochures, some PR, a little of everything. How about you?"

"I'll be in town till I get another assignment. Then I'll be off again. You know me." He shrugged and sipped his beer.

"Nice you could come back for a visit," she said, hoping she didn't sound insincere. "Bet your mom's happy to see you."

"She's here, too." He nodded toward the back door. "I left her in the kitchen trading recipes with your mom. Something about sponge cake."

"For Mom's strawberries," Francine said.

Anna Monroe and Olive Jarvis stepped from the house. Anna placed a large bowl on the buffet table and said, "Olive made her famous potato salad."

"Thank you, Olive," Luci said. Cody's mother was an attractive woman who shared her son's dark hair and brown eyes.

"You're most welcome." Olive enveloped Luci in a hug and then squeezed Anna's hand. "This is a happy day, isn't it? Both our children home again."

Cody rolled his eyes. "I'm going on thirty here."

"But children are always that, aren't they?"

"They are," Anna agreed.

"Well, look who's here!" Luci's father, having left his post at the barbecue pit, burst into the group, thrusting out his hand to Cody.

"Hey, Erv." Cody shook the other man's hand.

"Good to see you," Erv said. "Want to hear about all the places you've been."

Some of the other guests wandered over, and soon a large group had gathered around Cody. Luci edged away and circulated among the other guests, but Cody's presence distracted her. She heard him laugh politely at pharmacist Hal Barnett's corny joke and watched him help Don's wife, Arliss, pop open sodas for their children, ten-year-old Spencer and eight-year-old Hannah. She tracked his movements despite herself.

When her father's barbecued chicken was done, the guests lined up at the buffet table. Cody sat with Don and his family. Then Francine and her husband, Will, and their daughters, Betsy and Megan, joined the group. Luci thought about joining them but instead sat with two friends from high school and their families.

When Cody finished eating, he did what she expected him to do—put his camera into action. He gathered several couples and their children for a group shot. He caught her father and one of his golf buddies laughing over a joke, and her mother showing off her prize roses to the ladies in her garden club. Even the musicians posed for him.

Luci sighed. Cody had turned her homecoming party into one of his photo shoots.

Needing a break, she wandered to the edge of the lawn where a path led through the dunes to the beach. The ocean sparkled under a sun about to slip below the horizon, and the waves made a soft shushing sound as they rolled onto the shore. If only she could escape there now. When something upsetting happened, a walk on the beach always helped to calm her. Cody's unexpected appearance was certainly one of those times. As soon as the party was over...

"Luci."

She turned and, sure enough, there he stood, camera raised to his eye. He took a few shots and then backed away and took some more. Still more while down on one knee and yet another couple while standing with feet planted apart. Finally, he lowered the camera.

"Are you finished now?" Her words came out sharper than she'd intended. She must be in worse shape than she'd realized.

He frowned. "Not okay to take your picture? You're the guest of honor. Besides, you're a good subject."

"You didn't give me any warning. I probably need to comb my hair or something."

"Your hair is fine. The sunlight caught it just right." He tilted his head. "It's been—what?—a year since we've seen each other?"

"Yes, about that."

"Your last year at the U go okay?"

"It did."

She looked toward the water again—where the lowering sun spread rays of red, yellow and orange along the horizon—and wanted more than ever to take that walk on the beach. But the talk and laughter drifting across the lawn reminded her that the party offered an escape, too.

"I'd better get back to my guests," she said. "But thanks for coming, Cody, and good luck with your next assignment."

He laid a hand on her arm. "Don't say goodbye yet. I'll be around for a while. In a town as small as Willow Beach, we're bound to run into each other."

Just then, Don came toward them, waving his hand. "There you are, Cody. Been looking for you. Glen Thomas wants a word."

Cody raised his eyebrows. "The chamber of commerce president wants to talk to me? Why?"

Don shrugged. "Don't know. He didn't say."

"Okay," Cody said. "See you later, Luci."

"Sure. See you…later."

Luci hugged herself as she watched Cody and Don head back to the party. She'd thought she was telling the truth when she said she was over Cody. But the moment she laid eyes on him tonight, all her old feelings came rushing back.

Why did he have to return to Willow Beach, even for a short while, just when she was settling in again with her family and her new job?

CODY HEATED A mug of leftover coffee in the microwave and carried it to the table where his computer sat. His apartment—the detached garage on his mother's property—was the perfect quiet spot for reviewing photos. The living, dining and kitchen areas were one big room. His bedroom had an en suite bathroom, and he'd turned the second bedroom into a darkroom.

Cody sat at the table, put down his mug and clicked the mouse. A new picture flashed onto the screen. Another shot of Luci. He chuckled. He'd taken more pictures of her tonight than of anyone else.

She made a good subject. Her red hair always caught the light in unusual ways, sometimes reflecting blond highlights, other times a rich mahogany. Her hazel eyes were wide set and expressive, her nose straight and regal, and her mouth, with its full lower lip, was perfect.

He played with the photo, trying different filters to see their effects. At the same time, his thoughts lingered on the party. Luci's behavior puzzled him. Judging by her enthusiastic hug, she was glad to see him; but later, when he photographed her standing at the edge of the yard, she'd acted annoyed. Was her mood change related to the crush she'd had on him years ago? He thought she was over that.

He hadn't paid much attention to Luci when he and Don were in high school; she was just Don's kid sister. After graduation, Cody attended the University of Washington but dropped out after two years to work as a photographer for the *Willow Beach Herald*. A few years later, when Luci was a high school senior, she'd interned at the newspaper. Apparently, or so he'd been told by various people, that was when she'd developed her crush on him. He'd never encouraged her, not because he didn't like her, but because of the age difference. She was eighteen to his twenty-four.

After she graduated and he decided to finish his college education, they both ended up at the U. They got together a few times, nothing serious, just friends. On his part, anyway. Although the age difference wasn't as important anymore, by that time he'd wanted to travel the world as a freelance photographer.

He'd also decided on no romantic attachments. Asking a wife or a significant other to wait for him at home wouldn't be fair. Maybe someday he'd change his mind and want more. For now, he traveled *solamente*.

He'd expected Luci to move on, but he hadn't heard about a new guy in her life; nor had he seen anyone in particular hanging out with her tonight.

A knock sounded on his door. When he went to open it, his mother stood there, her arms full of towels and sheets.

"Sorry to interrupt your work," she said, "but I thought you could use some clean linens."

"You're not interrupting. I'm almost finished for the night. Come on in." He opened the door wider, and Olive swept in. "You don't have to do my laundry, you know." He closed the door behind her. "I'm a big boy now."

"I know, but I don't have that much laundry myself, so I might as well throw in yours." She looked around. "Where shall I put this?"

Cody pushed aside a bin full of photographs sitting on one of the tables. "Right here. I'll put them away later."

Olive set down the linens and then propped her hands on her hips and surveyed the room. "If you put any more equipment in here, you won't have space to turn around."

He looked around, trying to see the place as she saw it. Okay, the room was crowded. Several tables held computers, printers and scanners; tripods were propped in corners, and cameras, cases and other miscellaneous items filled the shelves. Enlargements of his photos decorated the walls.

"I like my place," he said. "It's cozy and has everything I need."

"Maybe so, but do you think you'll ever find a woman who'll put up with all this?" Olive went to the sofa and plumped up the loose cushions.

"Not a question that needs to be answered, because I'm not looking. Not right now, anyway."

"What about that woman who was on your

last assignment? The one you talked about in your emails?"

"Shar, from Omaha?" He smiled as the image of Sharlene Williams, with her blond hair and ready smile, popped into his mind. "Yeah, she's nice, but we're just friends."

Olive straightened and frowned at Cody. "Omaha is too far away, anyway. I always hoped you'd find someone closer to home."

Cody grinned at her wistful expression. "No woman would put up with my being gone most of the time. I'm—what do you old folks call it—a rolling stone."

Olive sighed. "Your dad really started something when he gave you that camera, didn't he?"

Cody chuckled and walked over to one of the shelves. "This one?" He picked up a child's red-and-yellow plastic camera. "Yeah, he did. And I was only, what, six?"

"Uh-huh. Right before he died." Olive's eyes misted. "And you'd go all over taking pictures, you with your little camera and he with his big one."

"Yep. And young as I was, I remember him telling me that when I got old enough, we'd travel the world and take lots and lots of pictures. 'Capturing the moment,' he called it, although I didn't understand what that meant." Cody's throat tightened. "We never got to do that."

"No, you didn't, and I'm so sorry. If only he could've beaten the cancer." She bit her lip and looked away.

Cody walked over to his mother and put his arm around her. "That's why I'm traveling now. I like to think he's with me on my trips, helping to capture the moments."

"That's a wonderful tribute, Cody. But what about passing on your love of photography to your son or daughter—wouldn't that also be a way to honor him?"

Cody smiled. "Ah, we're back to that again, are we?"

"You can't blame me for hoping." She cast him a sheepish look. "Some grandchildren would be nice."

"You have Emma's grandchildren." He replaced the camera on the shelf. "Think how lucky they are, having two grandmas to dote on them."

Olive and Emma Chester were lifelong friends. When Cody's father passed away, Cody and his mom had moved from Portland to Willow Beach, next door to Emma. One of the reasons Cody didn't worry about being gone so much was that his mom had Emma and her family for support.

"Emma's grands are sweet, but they're not the same as my own would be," she insisted, and then her expression brightened. "Anyway, it's nice to have you home, even if it's only for a week or so."

If Cody accepted Glen Thomas's offer, he'd be staying longer than a week. But could he handle it? Before long, the open road would be calling him again, like it always did.

CHAPTER TWO

"I DON'T SEE why you have to rent this apartment when you can live at home." Anna lifted a box from the family SUV and handed it to Luci.

"Mom, we've been over and over this issue." Luci took a deep breath and let it out slowly. "I want my own place. Simple as that. I'm only a couple miles away from you and Dad."

As much as Luci loved her parents, she needed her own apartment. Besides, she'd been living away from home for the past four years.

Before her mother could say more, Luci followed the stone walkway to unit six, where she set her box on the doorstep and unlocked the door. The aroma of fresh paint rushed to greet her. She picked up her box and stepped over the threshold. Her mother followed.

"Isn't this a cute place?" Luci set her load on an end table and made a sweeping gesture. "This is the living-dining room. That alcove is the kitchen, and there's the door to the bedroom and en suite bathroom."

Her mother set a box next to Luci's. "More like a motel than an apartment."

"It was a motel, Mom. Now, it's been remodeled and expanded into apartments. This will be my work space," she continued, indicating a large, rectangular table between the living area and the kitchen. "I'll put a file cabinet next to the table, and those cupboards underneath the counter will hold all my writing stuff."

"We have a real office you could use at home," Anna said.

Ignoring her mother's pointed comment, Luci crossed the room and opened the sliding glass door. "Come look at the patio."

Anna joined her, and they stepped onto a slab of cement furnished with two lawn chairs, a small, wrought-iron table and chairs, and several rectangular planter boxes. Cement walls on either side provided privacy from the neighbors.

"See how close I am to the ocean?" Luci

nodded to a path leading through the dunes to the shore. "I can take my daily walks, same as at home."

"Our house is closer to the beach and much more private. And what's in those planters? Looks like weeds." She walked over to inspect one box.

"You have my permission to plant something else."

"I'll see if I can spare something from my garden."

They finished unloading the SUV and Luci's car. Anna consulted her wristwatch. "I have a meeting with the garden club in fifteen minutes."

"Thanks for all your help today." Luci gave her mother a hug.

A smile softened Anna's tight lips. "You're so welcome, honey." She stepped back and snapped her fingers. "Oh, I almost forgot."

"What?"

"You'll see."

Anna dug into one of the boxes and pulled out a bowl Luci recognized. "For me? But that's your favorite bowl for your roses."

"I know, but you've always admired it and now it's yours."

"Oh, Mom." Luci's eyes misted as she ran her fingers over the bowl's yellow enameled surface. "Are you sure?"

"I am. It's a housewarming present. Or should I say 'apartment-warming'?"

"I'm honored. I'll put it here so I can admire it every day." She centered the bowl on the coffee table and gave her mother another hug. "Love you, Mom."

"Love you, too, darlin'. You'll have to excuse me today. It's hard to let go." Anna pulled a tissue from a pocket and dabbed at her eyes.

"I know. Me, too."

"Got to run now. Be sure to call if you need anything. And don't forget family Sunday."

"Of course not. I wouldn't miss dinner for anything."

Family Sunday had been a tradition for as long as Luci could remember. Once the kids started growing up and spending time away from home, her parents were adamant about maintaining the event. "We don't want you to forget you're part of this family," Ervin told them.

When Luci was away at university, they

hadn't expected her to attend, but now that she was back in Willow Beach, there would be no excuse.

Not that she'd ever offer one. Family was the main reason she'd come back to Willow Beach. As the youngest child, she'd had the love of her parents and her older brother and sister. Of course, they'd experienced the usual sibling rivalry, but underneath was a strong bond that kept them all together. And now that Don and Francine were married with children, there was an extended family. Luci looked forward to having her own family someday, knowing they would be welcomed and loved as much as she was.

After her mom left, Luci looked at the boxes and then at the open patio door. The door won. She could unpack later. Rummaging in her boxes of clothing, she located her favorite wide-brimmed hat. She put it on and tied the strings under her chin. Then she headed along the path through the dunes to the beach.

Once there, Luci tucked her hands in her sweater pockets and kept going. The beach was busy today. Some people were walking, like she was, while others jogged. Kids and dogs played in the surf, and on the hard-packed sand near the shore an occasional car or truck rumbled by.

A gull swooped down and landed in a large tide pool. Several more followed. The birds splashed and high stepped, poking their heads in and out of the water. It wasn't long—a few minutes at the most—before the leader spread its wings and flew into the sky. The others followed. Soon they were mere dots against the blue backdrop.

The birds reminded her of Cody. He never stayed in one place, either. Before long he swept off on a new adventure.

They were so different. He needed to keep moving, and she needed to stay still. Good thing they'd never gotten together. A relationship wouldn't work. Not then and not now.

MONDAY MORNING, JUST short of nine o'clock, Luci went through the glass double doors of the two-story Stafford Building, on the corner of Main and Seaview. Her heart fluttering, she followed the brightly lit, high-ceilinged hallway to the office of the chamber of commerce.

With her major in journalism, Luci could have applied for any number of positions. However, Willow Beach was a small town, and the opportunities were limited. Even the *Willow Beach Herald* had no openings. So she felt lucky to have found this job with the chamber of commerce.

Luci took a deep breath, then greeted the receptionist, Marge Delano.

Marge looked up from a desk piled with folders. "Luci, glad you're here. This mess belongs to you." She scooped up the folders and thrust them at Luci.

"Okay, but—" Luci juggled the folders to keep them anchored in her arms.

Marge made a dismissive wave. "Glen can explain. I'll let him know you're here."

She made a call, and a couple minutes later Glen Thomas appeared in the hallway.

Besides Luci's father, who was president of the Willow Beach National Bank, Glen was probably the only man in town who wore a tie to work. She'd bet there was a suit jacket in his office, too.

"Good morning, Luci," Glen boomed. "You're right on time. That's good. I like my staff to be punctual. So, let's get you started on your projects. Come this way, please." He motioned for her to follow him down the hall.

Luci's office turned out to be a large room with picture windows along one wall. She immediately looked out to see a courtyard with a fountain in the center. Colorful flower gardens and wooden benches surrounded the fountain. Two women sat drinking coffee in the sunshine.

Luci turned to Glen. "What a pleasant setting."

"Mmm, yes, I suppose it is." He pointed to a table stacked with file folders, magazines and brochures. "You can put those files Marge gave you with the rest of that stuff. It all goes together."

Luci deposited her armload on the table, then sat and took her tablet from her purse.

"Nice party the other night." Glen pulled up a chair across from her.

"I'm glad you and your wife could join us." Luci turned on her tablet, ready to take notes.

"Your dad and I go way back, you know. We both came to town about the same time. He worked at the bank, and I worked at the hardware store. Now he's the bank's president, and I'm owner of the store and president of the chamber of commerce." He chuckled. "How about that?"

"I'd say you've both done very well for yourselves."

He nodded and stroked his chin. "I wasn't sure I'd like living in such a small town, but it hasn't been so bad, after all. The place kinda grows on you."

"Yes, it does."

"Well. We'd better get moving." He tapped his wristwatch. "Have to meet with the mayor soon. There's a list for you somewhere around here. At least, Marge said there would be." He poked around the piles and came up with a piece of paper. "Ah, here it is." He took a pair of eyeglasses from his shirt pocket and put them on.

"You'll be writing an article each month for *Coastal Living* magazine. It's published in Hampton, but the surrounding towns all contribute stories." He gave her a questioning look over the top of his glasses.

"I'm familiar with *Coastal Living*." Luci made a note on her tablet.

"Good. The next issue is out the first of July, so you'll need to turn in your article soon. The person who last had this job planned to write about Cranberry Acres. I suggest you follow through on that."

"I'll make it a priority."

He pointed to another item on the list. "The Fourth of July celebration. That's taken care of by the outfit we hire to do the fireworks display. You'll need to do some publicity, though, flyers around town, that sort of thing."

Luci nodded, busily taking notes.

Mr. Thomas took off his glasses and dangled them between thumb and forefinger. "Now, here's a real challenge. The sand-castle contest in August. We want to add something new this year, something that will get us a lot of attention. You decide what that will be. Make us look good."

"Okay..."

He replaced his glasses and consulted the list again. "The newsletter to our members. Published twice a month."

"All right."

He put down the list and gestured to the stacks of papers and folders on the table.

"Then, there's all this stuff. Needs to be sorted and put in those file cabinets over there." He nodded at several cabinets standing side by side on the far wall. "A lot of the brochures need to be updated. You can do that, too."

He waited while Luci keyed in a few more notes. "How're we doing here? Any questions?"

"Yes. For the articles and the brochure updates, will you want me to take photos, too? I'm not a professional, of course, but—"

"Photos won't be your responsibility. Our regular guy, Sam Reynolds, is on an extended vacation, but I've hired someone to fill in."

A knock sounded on the open door. Glen looked up. "Here he is now."

When Luci turned to see who had arrived, shock rippled through her. "Cody?"

He waved. "Hi, Luci. Glen."

"Have a seat." Glen motioned to a chair across from Luci. "And you call me Glen, too, Luci. No need to be formal."

Cody, looking neat and trim in a short-sleeved plaid shirt and jeans, ambled across the room. He pulled out a chair next to Glen, sat and stretched his long legs underneath the table. Of course, his camera was with him, slung over his shoulder.

Glen continued talking, but his words barely registered. All Luci could think about was that she and Cody would be working together. Was she his boss now?

"Cody, you can set your own office hours," Glen was saying, "just so long as you meet all the deadlines. Luci, I'll expect you to be here most of the time, except when you're out doing research, of course." He looked at his watch. "Ah, time for the mayor. I'll let you two get started."

After Glen left, neither Cody nor Luci said anything. She fussed with her tablet while he folded his arms and leaned back in his chair. The seconds ticked by.

Finally Cody cleared his throat. "I get the feeling you're not happy with this situation."

Luci put down her tablet and idly picked up one of the brochures. "I'm surprised. No, shocked. Why would you want this job? I thought you were eager to be off to see the world again."

"I am. But when Glen offered me the job, I decided to take it. I won't be stuck here long. At the end of the summer, Sam Reynolds will be back, and by then I'll have a new assignment. In the meantime, I could use the money."

Money. Why hadn't she thought of that? Of course, his accepting Glen's offer didn't have anything to do with her. Not that she wanted it to.

"We worked together at the *Herald*," Cody said.

She slid the brochure away and snatched at another one. "A few times, and I was an intern then—still in high school, for goodness' sake. This is different."

"Don't worry, Luci, we'll be fine." He leaned forward. "So, what's first on the agenda?"

"An article about Cranberry Acres for *Coastal Living*. We'll need to make a trip there for an interview and photos."

"Sounds good. I'll let you work out the details. Meanwhile, how about going for a coffee?"

"Ah, no thanks. I really need to stay here and get acquainted with my new office. I'll have some later." *I really need to be alone for a while.*

His brow furrowed, and she braced herself for an argument.

Instead, he said, "All right, call or text me when you've got something for me to do."

"You're really going to take orders from me?"

"Well…that depends. I pretty much do my own thing when it comes to taking pictures. But, like I said, we can make this work."

She narrowed her eyes. "You think?"

"We have to. This job is important for both of us."

After Cody left, Luci leaned back and closed her eyes. She didn't share his confidence that they could work together. If only she could get rid of her feelings for him. Feelings she didn't understand. Did she still have a crush on him? No, she didn't think so. Then what? Was she in love with him? What would be the use of that? He obviously wasn't in love with her, and their goals and lifestyles were so far apart.

She squared her shoulders and lifted her chin. This was her dream—coming home after graduation, being a part of her wonderful family and having a job she loved. She wasn't going to let Cody Jarvis spoil her joy.

He'd be here for the summer, and then he'd be gone again and out of her life forever.

JUST BEFORE NOON, Cody headed to Charlie's Fish House, a favorite of his. Charlie's hadn't changed since he'd last been there. The same plain wooden tables and chairs, the same counter with red vinyl stools, the same chalkboard menu hanging on the wall.

As he stood in line to place his order, he heard a familiar voice behind him say, "Well, look who's here."

He turned to see Luci's older brother, Don. "Hey, what's the banker doing at Charlie's? I'd expect you to choose someplace like the Beach Café."

"Not unless I'm entertaining clients. How come you're by yourself?"

"First day on the job, and Luci didn't want to leave the office."

Don stuck his hands in his pockets and rocked back on his heels. "Ah, so you accepted Glen's job offer."

"I did. The money will come in handy."

"Having you in town for a while will be like old times. Wanna share a table?"

"Sure."

When they got to the front of the line, Cody chose the fish-fries-chowder combo, a house specialty. They took their tickets and sat at a window table. Other diners filled the deck, and on the beach below, several kids played volleyball while two golden Labrador retrievers chased each other around the dunes. Cody let his gaze wander over the scene, automatically framing pictures. After lunch, he'd take a walk on the beach and capture some of the action.

"So, how's your first day going?" Don asked.

Cody shrugged. "Glen's a little full of himself, but I can deal with him. I'm more worried about your sister. She's not happy with the situation. Maybe she's decided she doesn't like me."

Don's grin turned sly. "The problem is she likes you too much."

Cody jerked to attention. "Say what?"

"You heard me. You might see clearly through that lens—" he pointed to Cody's camera "—but without it, you're kinda nearsighted."

Cody shook his head. "Are you sure? I

know she had a crush on me years ago, but she's over that, right?"

"I don't think so."

"Did she actually tell you that?"

"Ah, no."

"Did she tell anyone you know? Francine? Arliss? Your parents?"

"Not that I know of." Don spread his hands. "But, trust me, I know my sister and what goes on in her mind. Well, most of the time."

Cody waved that aside. "Anyone who says they know what goes on in a woman's mind is kidding themselves."

Don laughed. "You can think what you want, and I'll know what I know."

A waiter arrived with their orders, and for the next few minutes, food claimed Cody's attention. He started with the chowder, which was as good as he remembered: the sauce rich and thick and loaded with clams, bite-size potatoes and bits of bacon.

When he came up for air, he looked at the hamburger on Don's plate. "You're having a burger when there's all this great seafood?"

Don took a sip of his Coke and set down the glass. "Arliss is on a fish kick. After three nights of salmon—broiled, loafed and quiched—I'm ready for a change."

"She's gonna keep you healthy."

"She's trying, anyway."

Cody sliced off a piece of fish and popped it into his mouth. "Married life agrees with you," he said when he'd chewed and swallowed. "Never would have thought it. And your job, too. Look at you, all dressed for the part." He nodded at Don's blue dress shirt and tan slacks.

Don laughed and then sobered. "Maybe so, but I told Dad no tie. Never."

"He still wear one?"

Don rolled his eyes. "Oh, yeah. But at his age, he can be excused. Tell you the truth, though, I'd rather be fishing."

"Are you sorry you followed your dad into the world of finance?"

Don looked away. When he turned back to Cody, his eyes were troubled. "Yes, I am sorry."

Cody grimaced. "That's a shame. You worked hard to be where you are."

"I know." Don put a finger to his lips. "So don't tell the old man. The money's good, and it comes in handy when you have a wife and two kids, which I wouldn't trade for anything, mind you."

"Well, I'm glad you and Arliss are happy together."

"For sure. But marriage is not for guys like you."

Cody dipped a French fry into the ketchup on his plate. "What do you mean, 'guys like me'?"

"You're not a nester."

Cody wrinkled his nose. "A what?"

"A nester. You need to settle down someplace, especially if you plan to have kids. That's what Arliss said before we were married. 'Where's our nest, honey?'"

"Huh, the only nests I get close to are filled with birds."

Don laughed. "Figures."

"So, back to Luci. You don't mind that we're working together when she's got a thing for me? I'd think you'd want to protect her."

Don put his burger on his plate and leaned forward. "Have you met my sister? She's got a mind of her own. You don't mess with her. But in your situation, she writes and you take pictures. You're a winning combo."

"Sure. We'll be working together. That's all."

Don shrugged and picked up his burger again. "That's up to you."

Cody finished his meal and wiped his lips with his napkin. "Why do I feel like she and I are some sort of experiment you're all watching? Lab rats or something."

"Your mind is weird, my friend. I'll have to think on that. Just don't hurt my sister, okay?"

Cody raised both hands. "Of course I won't. You've got my word on that."

"Just kidding. I know you wouldn't."

When they were on their way out of the restaurant, Don said, "You still going fishing with me and Max on Saturday?"

"I'm looking forward to it."

Max Billings was another friend from high school. The three of them fished a lot back then, and when Cody was in town, they kept up that tradition.

"Great. Max is bringing a new guy in town, Ben somebody."

Cody gave a thumbs-up. "As they say, the more, the merrier."

Don headed back to work, and Cody went

to the beach, his thoughts centered on Luci. If she still had feelings for him, maybe their working together this summer wasn't such a good idea. Maybe he should've turned down Glen's offer.

But he did need the money. He had a few checks coming in from some freelance jobs, but not a steady salary. Not that he wanted steady. He didn't want to be tied down, day after day doing the same thing, with the same people, in the same place. That routine might work for some, but not him.

A shout from teenagers playing Frisbee caught his attention. The orange disc sailed high into the air, and their cocker spaniel leaped after it. Cody grabbed his camera and went to work. Fifteen minutes later, after the kids ambled off down the beach, he sat on a log reviewing what he'd captured. One photo caught a boy with his hand outstretched, having just let go of the disc. Another showed the dog snagging the Frisbee in its mouth. The other pictures brought a smile to his lips, too. This was what he was born to do. And wasn't that what life was all about? Discovering what you were meant to do and then doing it?

CHAPTER THREE

"How much farther?" Cody asked, drumming on his SUV's steering wheel.

Luci consulted the map on her cell phone. "Looks like a couple more miles before we reach the turnoff."

"Okay. I'll keep an eye out."

Three days had passed since Luci and Cody began working together. Actually, they hadn't really talked since that first day. She'd spent the time familiarizing herself with her office and the routine, and Cody had been in and out, doing some special photography work for Glen.

Today, they were on their way to interview Ray Dunbar, owner of Cranberry Acres, for the article in *Coastal Living*. They'd left Willow Beach behind and driven through a countryside dotted with farmhouses and fields where cows and horses grazed.

Luci would have enjoyed the trip more if

she'd been alone—or if she'd been with any-one other than Cody. She had no idea how they would work together in this new ar-rangement. Would he be a good partner? Or would he be off doing his own thing?

Just being near him was disconcerting. Like now—barely a foot separated them. She was so aware of him. Today he wore a blue T-shirt that showed off his broad chest and muscular arms. He still hadn't had a haircut, and the ends were beginning to curl.

The SUV lurched as Cody made a quick turn to the right. "Almost missed the turnoff. I thought you were watching."

"I was, ah, thinking about my interview questions."

"You've got them all written out, I bet." He checked his mirrors and continued driv-ing down the new road.

"Of course I do. Don't you plan what pic-tures you're going to take when you're on an assignment?"

"Not so much. I like to be spontaneous. Life is out there. Let it happen and look for the moment."

"The moment, huh?"

He took his gaze off the road long enough to shoot her a quick grin. "Yeah. That special moment in time that I'll capture forever with my camera."

"Must be nice. For an interview, I need to have a plan." She held up her notebook.

"Nothing wrong with a plan. But open yourself up to being spontaneous, too." Catching her frown, he added, "Hey, I'm only trying to be helpful. I've been in this business longer than you."

Luci pressed her lips together. "I know, but I do have my degree now, with a lot of field experience behind it. That ought to be worth something."

"Sure, Luci. Just some friendly advice."

Luci fell silent. How was she supposed to do her job with him micromanaging her?

At Cranberry Acres, a woman in the office gave them directions, and they found Ray Dunbar rinsing out buckets under a faucet. Besides the wide-brimmed leather hat the woman had told them to look for, he wore a plaid shirt and khaki work pants. His knee-high rubber boots were caked with mud.

He turned off the water and studied Luci. "Ervin Monroe's daughter, right?"

"I am." His flat tone gave no indication whether that was an asset or a liability.

"So you're working for Glen this summer."

"Not just for the summer. I'm back in Willow Beach for good."

"I see." He hooked the bucket handle on the faucet and shifted his attention to Cody. "And you're—"

"Cody Jarvis. I'm the summer help."

Ray pulled off his work gloves, and he and Cody shook hands. "Either of you ever visit the farm before?" he asked.

Cody nodded. "When I was in grade school, my class came here on a field trip."

"Mine, too," Luci added. "But I'm sure I'll have a different perspective now."

Ray nodded. "Growing and harvesting cranberries is an involved operation. But let me give you a tour, and I'll explain the process as simply as I can."

Ray led them to the troughs where the cranberries grew. Having taken out her tablet, Luci asked him the questions she'd listed. Keeping his promise to make his explanation simple, Ray's answers were short and to the point. The berries were planted in April or

May and harvested in mid-October. Most of the harvest was made into juice.

"I'd like a few pictures of you," Luci said after she'd got what she needed for the article. She looked around for Cody. He was nowhere in sight. Her temper simmered. Why couldn't he stay nearby while she was interviewing their subject?

Ray consulted his wristwatch. "We'll have to make it quick—I need to leave for a meeting in a few minutes."

"Sure. Just as soon as I can find my, ah, associate." Finally, she spotted Cody on the other side of the field, aiming his camera at the top of a pine tree. What did a pine tree have to do with cranberries?

She caught his eye and waved him over. He took his time, pausing twice to aim his camera at something, she wasn't sure what. Her cheeks were burning, and she struggled to paste a smile on her face. Ray paced, checking his watch again.

"Ray has to leave for another meeting," she said when Cody finally joined them. "And we need his photo."

"Oh, sorry, I didn't know—" Cody wrinkled his forehead.

Ray made a dismissive wave. "It's okay. But let's get a move on."

Later, on their way back to Willow Beach, Luci stared out the window at the passing landscape. The interview had left her nerves ragged.

Cody broke the silence. "Did I drive you crazy?"

"Just about," she said, only half kidding. "This job means a lot to me, you know."

"I do know. And I take my work seriously, too. We just have different approaches. You like to have a plan, and I like to be spur-of-the-moment."

"Maybe so, but it would've helped if you'd hung around while I was interviewing him. There wasn't time for as many photos of him as I'd hoped."

"Oh, I don't know. I'll bet that of the ones I took, you'll find some that will work. And I can't wait to read what you write about him. If I had to describe him, I'd probably say something like 'tall dude with big leather hat.'"

Despite her annoyance, Luci giggled. "Yeah, I can just see that in the article. Glen would have a fit."

"Maybe you should try something offbeat sometime. Well, not that offbeat, but you get the idea."

When they returned to the office, Cody pulled into the parking lot. Leaving the engine running, he turned to her. "Want to go over the photos I took?"

"Yes, but I'd like to have a rough draft of the text before we sit down together. How about tomorrow afternoon?"

"Sure. I have another project I'm working on, too. Something I think you'll be interested in."

LUCI SAT BACK in her desk chair and read the paragraph she'd just written. The article on Cranberry Acres was taking shape, but she still wasn't ready for Cody's input. And here it was, Friday already. When she'd returned to the office yesterday, Glen had summoned her for an impromptu meeting with some of the people involved in the Fourth of July celebration, and it had lasted until quitting time. At home, she'd spent most of the evening reviewing Cody's pictures—there were quite a few—and did little writing.

She checked her wristwatch. Only an hour before quitting time. She could stay late, but if she were going to work overtime, she'd rather do it at home. But what about Cody?

She called him, breathing a sigh of relief when he answered the phone. She explained her predicament, ending with, "The deadline's Monday, so that doesn't give us much time."

"You're almost done, you say?"

"I think so. I'll know better when we finalize the photos."

He let a beat go by and then said, "Why don't I come over to your place tonight? Unless you have a date?"

"Ah, no. My only date is with the article."

"How about seven o'clock?"

"Well…okay. I'm at the Driftwood, number six."

"See you then."

AT A QUARTER to seven that evening, Luci stood in front of the bathroom mirror brushing her hair. She put down the brush and peered at her image. Should she wear lipstick or go natural? Did her sweater look ratty? Or casual and comfortable? Finally, she came to her senses. What was wrong with her? This wasn't a date—this was work. She didn't have to fix herself up for Cody.

He arrived promptly at seven and breezed in, carrying a white paper bag in one hand and a small black box in the other. He handed her the paper bag.

"What's this?" she asked and then spotted the Bon Ton Bakery logo. She peeked into the bag. "Ah, doughnuts. Chocolate frosted." Her mouth was watering already.

"There's strawberry, too. I trust you have coffee to go with."

"I do. Good thing I made a big pot." She pointed to the box. "What else did you bring?"

He patted the top. "This is for later, when we're through working." He set the box on the coffee table.

"I have the article up on the computer. Why don't you take a look while I put these dough-nuts on a plate and pour us some coffee?"

"Got to check your view first." He walked to the patio door and looked out.

"Don't you want to take a picture or two?"

she asked. Of course, his camera was slung around his neck.

"Maybe later," he said with a good-natured grin.

By the time she had set the doughnuts and coffee on the table and pulled up a chair beside him, he was deep into reading the article. While he finished, she munched a doughnut and sipped her coffee. Finally, he sat back and frowned. Uh-oh. Her stomach knotted.

"So what do you think?"

He nodded and reached for a doughnut, brushing against her shoulder in the process. "I think it's pretty darn good."

"No, I hear something else in your voice. What?"

He studied the screen again, scrolling up and down. "It might be a little stiff."

"Stiff? What does that mean?"

"A few more quotes from Dunbar might liven it up."

She put down her mug and folded her arms. "He wasn't the most talkative person."

"I know. Forget I said anything. Why'd you ask me, anyway?"

"I wanted, ah…" What did she want? His approval? He wasn't her boss.

But he was her partner. They were in this job together, for better or worse. "I'll give quotes some thought."

"And the photos of Dunbar. They turned out all right, didn't they? How about that shot where he's cupping one of the plants in his hands? I thought that showed how much he cares about his plants."

"I do like that one."

"But what about the one where he's standing and gazing at the bogs. It's a good one, too, even if he has a poker face."

She had to smile. "He did, didn't he? Hmm." She skimmed the article. "I don't see a spot for it, though."

"How about here?" He pointed to a line on the screen.

"No, no, doesn't fit."

They went back and forth for a while without reaching an agreement. Finally, Cody threw up his hands. "I think we're done here. But give my suggestions some more thought, okay?"

"Sure." *Maybe.*

Luci turned off the computer. She picked

up their coffee mugs and carried them to the sink. He followed with the plate of leftover doughnuts.

"Thanks for coming—and for your help." She took the plate and placed it beside the mugs.

"You're welcome, but we're not done yet."

"I thought you just said we were?"

"Nope. One more thing." He held out his hand. "Come on."

Luci stared for a moment and then, with an inward sigh, held out her hand and let their fingers mesh. He led her to the sofa, and while she sat he picked up the box he'd brought and held it out.

"What this?"

"Something I made for you. Go on, open it."

She pulled off the lid. Inside lay a book. "Luci's Homecoming" was printed on the cover, and below that a photo of her smiling face.

"From my party. Oh, Cody…"

He sat next to her, and they paged through the album, looking at all the photos he'd taken that night. "There's Don mugging for the camera," she said. "And there's Dad with his arm around Mom."

"They sure look happy. Married how long?"

"Thirty-three years next March."

He'd managed to capture the children in cute poses, and all the other guests, too. There were even photos of the ocean view and the sunset.

When they finished looking at the pictures, Luci closed the cover and turned to Cody. "Thank you. What a wonderful gift."

"You're welcome. I made books for your parents, and for Don and Francine, too."

"I'm sure they'll appreciate them as much as I do. And I'm sorry I was such a brat about your taking my picture that night."

He made a dismissive wave. "No problem. I know you weren't expecting me to show up for your homecoming."

She laughed. "You were a surprise, all right."

They turned toward each other, and their eyes met. Warmth flooded her face and her heart thudded. Swallowing hard, she tore her gaze away.

Cody cleared his throat. "Say, what time

is it?" He checked his wristwatch. "Nine, already? Gotta be on my way. Early get up tomorrow. Fishing trip with your brother and Max."

In no time at all, he was at the door. His hand on the knob, he turned and said, "Glad the article's done. You did good, kid." He gave her a pat on the shoulder, and then he was gone.

After he left, Luci dropped onto the sofa and put her head in her hands. The evening had worn her out. Okay, they'd managed to put together the article, but it hadn't been easy. He thought that he knew best just because he had more experience. But she was the boss here, wasn't she?

CODY GRIPPED HIS fishing rod while the *Half Time* bucked another wave and water sloshed onto the deck. Good thing he'd brought his waterproof camera. Don was sitting next to him, also keeping a tight hold on his fishing rod.

On the other side of the boat were Max Billings and the new guy, Ben Shapiro. The *Half Time*'s owner and captain, Ole Swenson, rounded out their party.

Don suddenly leaned back as his rod arced and the line went taut. "I got one!"

Max looked over his shoulder. "Keep your line tight," he said.

"Must be a big one," Ben put in.

Standing at the helm, Ole grinned and gave a thumbs-up. He idled the engine, which sent the boat plunging into the waves and water splashing onto the deck. Cody anchored his reel and grabbed his camera. This was a photo op not to be missed.

Don's face turned red and his breath huffed. Max yelled orders. Ben looked on as though awed by the whole thing.

"There he is!" Max pointed.

Sure enough, a king salmon burst into view, its silver scales catching the sun's rays. Then the fish plunged back into the water. Don reeled more line. The boat rocked and rolled.

"Here he comes!" Don yelled.

The fish broke the waves again and for a moment, tail swinging, hung suspended in the air. Cody caught that moment and several more. Then it was all over, and Don's prize catch lay on the deck.

Not for long, though. Ole packed the fish in

ice while the others talked about what a great catch it was, and Cody reviewed his shots. Don may have caught the king salmon, but for Cody, his pictures were much more valuable than any fish. The shot of the salmon in midair was exactly what he'd hoped for. He could already see the photo blown up and hanging on a wall or featured on a magazine cover.

Before the trip was over, they'd each landed a salmon, although none were as big as Don's. Back in the marina, they posed for photos with their prizes and got a ritual picture to take home and show to friends, along with a story that would be embellished each time it was told.

After making arrangements to pick up their fish later, they celebrated at the marina's tavern. The group sat on the deck, watching the other charters drift in like hunters coming home.

The marina was close to Smuggler's Cove, where bootleggers had hidden their stashes during Prohibition. Willow Beach was full of interesting history, but, with the entire world calling, Cody had never taken the time to pursue it. Maybe someday.

During a lull in the conversation, Cody turned his attention to the newcomer. "So, Ben, you're from Seattle?"

Ben sipped his beer and set down the glass. "Right. Thought I might like living on the coast."

"And you're an accountant."

"Yep, a numbers cruncher. I opened an office in the Stafford Building. Already have a fair number of clients."

"Including us," Max said. "That's how me 'n' Ben got acquainted." Max was a partner in Fuller's Foods, Willow Beach's main grocery and variety store.

Cody couldn't imagine staring at numbers all day, but someone had to do it. Ben looked the part, with his blond hair neatly cut and jaw clean shaven. While Cody, Max and Don were dressed in sloppy shirts and faded jeans, Ben wore a sports shirt that was molded to his chest and tucked into jeans that somehow had a crease.

He seemed a nice enough guy, though, and he might appeal to Luci. Since Cody had heard that Luci still had a thing for him, he'd been trying to figure out what he could do—without hurting her. He'd decided that she needed another guy to catch her interest. Then she would forget about him. Maybe Ben could be that guy.

"You attached?" he asked Ben, in what he hoped was a casual tone.

"Am I married, you mean? No."

"Girlfriend? Significant other?"

"Not at the moment."

"Me, neither." Cody chuckled. "Lucky us, huh?"

Don jumped into the conversation. "Do I hear you bad-mouthing the holy state of matrimony? It's not so bad, is it, Max?"

Max folded his arms over his brawny chest. "You'll have to ask Trixie about that."

Don smirked. "Yeah, Arliss and I saw you two the other night at the movies, holding hands like you were on your first date."

"A night out without the kids is a date," Max said. "And Trixie insists on one date night a month." He shrugged. "I can't complain."

Ben made no comment. He didn't appear to be much of a talker. But then, Cody often became an observer, too, always keeping an eye out for the next picture. Like now. He spotted a gull about to land on the piling at the mouth of the harbor. *Look at that wing-span. Look at the angle. Look at the legs come down. Must be like landing a plane.* He picked up his camera.

Later, on the way to their vehicles, Cody caught up with Ben. "Good to have you along today."

Ben nodded. "Catching that fish made my day."

They turned into the parking lot, dodging a couple cars and stepping onto the path. "You probably don't know many people in town yet, being new and all."

"Haven't had much time. Busy lining up clients. And bird-watching. That's one of the reasons I moved here. I'm an amateur orni-thologist."

"That so? I've been known to stalk a few birds myself." At Ben's startled look, he added, "When I'm taking pictures. You know." He let a moment go by while some others passed them on the path and then con-tinued, "A friend of mine works in the same building you do. I could introduce you, if you're interested."

Ben's forehead wrinkled, but then he said, "Well…okay."

"Super. Give me a day or so to work out the particulars, and I'll get back to you."

Ben nodded and pulled his car keys from his pocket. "Sounds like a plan."

Cody climbed into his SUV and headed out of the marina lot. Ben had been a whole lot easier to reel in than the fish he'd caught today. Now, he had to find the right time to get him and Luci together.

Cody pasted a big grin on his face and wore it all the way home.

CHAPTER FOUR

"Did you submit your article on Cranberry Acres to *Coastal Living*?" Glen asked.

Luci put down the brochure advertising a charter boat service and sat back in her chair. She'd managed to organize some of the material, but countless stacks remained. The mess was driving her crazy.

"I did turn in the article. I haven't had a response yet from the editor."

"It looked good to me." Glen hitched up his trousers over his ample stomach. The day was a warm one, and he'd shed his jacket and rolled up his shirtsleeves, but the ever-present tie adorned his neck. "But then, what do I know about it? That's why I hired you and Cody. By the way, have you seen him lately?"

"Not since we went over the article together. I'm working on the brochures now, picking out the ones that need updating. When I get them organized, I'll contact him to take some photos." Not that she'd be picking up the phone anytime soon. Working together or not, seeing Cody as little as possible suited her just fine.

"Good, good." Glen idly picked up a brochure from one of the stacks she'd assembled, riffled through it and then tossed it onto the table. "But don't forget about the sand-castle contest."

Luci retrieved the brochure and carefully put it where it belonged. "Of course. I've been giving it a lot of thought."

He frowned. "You need to do more than that, Luci. You need to come up with an idea. A brilliant one. We need a new twist this year. Make us look good."

Not long after Glen left, Marge rushed in, her arms loaded with yellow file folders. She dumped them onto the worktable, where they slid into the neat piles of brochures.

"Oops, sorry." Marge leaned over the table, scrambling to corral the files.

"What's all this?" Luci rescued the brochures and set them aside.

"Cleaning out more files." Marge straightened and waved her arms. "Not my idea. Glen's orders. This is stuff from decades ago.

If it was up to me—" she thumbed her chest "—I'd toss it. But now that you're here, he wants everything organized and up-to-date." She rolled her eyes. "Pressure, pressure."

The phone in the outer office rang.

"That's probably the mayor," Marge said. "Gotta go." She scurried out the door.

After Marge left, Luci abandoned the brochures and the rest of the mess on the worktable and migrated to her computer to research sand-castle contests.

She was deep into her work when Cody arrived.

Another man accompanied him. The newcomer looked vaguely familiar, like someone she might have passed in the hallway. He wasn't as tall as Cody, but then most men weren't. He was dressed in neatly pressed slacks and a plaid shirt that looked, well, sprayed on. His blond hair was cut short and combed back from a high forehead.

"Luci, meet Ben Shapiro." Cody gestured to his companion. "He's new in town. An accountant. Has an office upstairs."

"Pleased to meet you, Luci."

Ben offered her a shy smile along with

his outstretched hand. But his fingers barely touched hers before he drew back.

"I thought I'd seen you here in the building. Welcome to Willow Beach," Luci said.

"Thanks." Ben broke eye contact and looked around.

"Ben's also a bird fancier," Cody put in. "That's one of the reasons he moved here from Seattle. Right, Ben?"

"Right."

Ben seemed to have found something interesting on the ceiling, although Luci couldn't imagine what that was. "We do have a lot of birds here on the coast," she said.

No one spoke for a couple of seconds, and then Cody snapped his fingers. "Say, if we do an article on birds for *Coastal Living*, maybe you could be our go-to guy. Have you seen that mag, Ben? You got a copy handy, Luci?"

"I do, somewhere around here." Luci rummaged through a stack of papers on her desk and pulled out a copy of the magazine. She held it out to Ben.

He riffled through the pages. "Yes, I've seen this around town."

"And didn't you say you'd written some

articles yourself?" Cody asked. "For professional journals? Birds something-or-other?"

Ben looked up from the magazine. "*Birds of the West Coast* and *Birdology*."

Luci hadn't heard of either of those publications, but, when nothing more was forthcoming from Ben, she said, "Oh? If you have extra copies, I'd love to read them."

Cody nodded. "Might give us some ideas."

"Sure. I have some extra copies." He handed the magazine back to Luci and looked at his wristwatch. "I gotta get back to the office. Client coming in a few minutes. Pleased to meet you, Luci."

He finally made eye contact, along with a small nod.

"You, too, Ben."

Cody walked to the door with Ben. "Don't be a stranger now, you hear?"

Ben mumbled a reply, but Luci couldn't make out the words.

She sat at her desk, ready to resume her work. Cody returned and stood over her, arms folded across his chest.

"So what do you think?"

She looked up. "About what? The article idea?"

"Ah, yeah. About that."

"It has possibilities."

Cody paced a few steps and then turned. "How about Ben? What do you think about him?"

"You mean as a resource person?"

"Resource. Sure."

"I don't know. I'll have to talk to him some more. Except he doesn't say much, does he?"

"He might be a little shy."

Luci narrowed her eyes. "Cody, what is going on here?"

"Ben went fishing with us on Saturday. He's Max's accountant. And when he mentioned he was interested in birds, I thought maybe he'd be a good contact."

"Uh-huh."

"Okay, since he's new in town and, as you saw, shy, I thought he could use some help getting to know people… Say, I gotta run, too. Glen's got an assignment for me. Do you have anything? I can come back later."

"I will have something on the sand-castle contest…soon. I'll let you know."

Luci watched Cody hurry out the door. He was acting strangely today. But she didn't have time to worry about him now.

She had a job to do. She turned back to her computer and her research.

ANXIOUS TO GET away from Luci's questions, Cody headed down the hall to Glen's office. Had he been too obvious? This matchmaking stuff was harder than he'd thought it would be. Still, he'd gotten the ball rolling, and he wasn't about to give up.

The following day, Luci mentioned that Ben had dropped off copies of his articles and she had given him some brochures on the Wildlife Refuge. She made no mention of getting together with Ben after hours, though, and Cody didn't want to raise her suspicions any further by inquiring. He waited a couple more days, and when no progress appeared to have been made, he figured he'd have to give Ben another nudge.

He was at the post office when he spotted Ben pulling mail from a postal box. They exchanged greetings and a bit of small talk, and then Cody got down to business.

"What'd you think of Luci?" he asked.

Ben tucked his mail into his jacket pocket. "She's very knowledgeable about writing. We talked a bit when I gave her my articles."

Cody nodded. "Talking's good. But what did you think of her? She's attractive, isn't she?"

"Very. You on your way out?" Ben gestured toward the door. "I need to get back to the office."

"Yeah, I'm done here." They fell into step walking across the marble floor to the open door, dodging people along the way. "Luci was an intern at the *Herald* when I worked there. Then we went to the U at the same time, although I graduated a year ahead of her."

"So you two go way back."

"Just as friends." Cody emphasized the word *friends*.

They went down the steps to the parking lot. Cody was searching his brain for something else to say about Luci when Ben asked, "Is she seeing anyone?"

Finally. He was beginning to think he'd have to spell it out. "No, she's not. She was dating a guy at the U for a while, but that didn't work out." Cody was glad it hadn't. Seth had seemed like a loser. Not good enough for Luci. He eyed Ben. Was he good enough?

"So, you think you'd like to ask Luci out?"

Ben nodded. "I was thinking of asking her to dinner."

Yes! Cody restrained himself from making a fist and pumping the air and instead nodded solemnly. "I'm sure she'd like that."

"Where would you suggest we go? I could ask her for suggestions, but I'd like to have some ideas myself." Ben whipped out a pair of sunglasses from his jacket pocket and pushed them up on his nose with his forefinger.

"Beach Café's probably your best bet. Casual but with a touch of elegance. Can't beat the view." He was already imagining them at a window table, enjoying one of Willow Beach's spectacular sunsets—when they weren't gazing into each other's eyes.

Ben took out his car keys. "Sounds good. Why don't you come, too?"

Cody gave him a look. "Me?" He pointed at himself. "Why would I—"

Ben shrugged. "I'm not much of a talker… In fact, maybe this isn't such a good idea, after all."

"No, wait." Cody put out a hand. "Okay, I'll come and…bring someone." Right now, he had no idea who. But if that was what it took to get Ben and Luci together, he'd do it.

Ben looked at his watch. "Gotta go. I'm late."

Before Cody could say any more, Ben climbed into his truck. He started the engine and roared from the parking lot.

Cody stared after him. What had just happened here? But maybe his presence on their date would be a good thing. Then he could make sure Ben and Luci were getting along okay.

But now he had to come up with someone for himself. Who would that be? Most of the women he knew were either married or had moved away. He wandered down Main Street, deep in thought.

He was about to give up when he found himself in front of Sylvie's Souvenir Shop. Sylvie Ventura. He snapped his fingers. Yes.

He opened the door and went inside. "Is Sylvie around?" he asked the teenage clerk.

She nodded toward the back of the store. "In the office."

Cody hurried past the crowded shelves. Seashells were everywhere: wind chimes, boxes, lamps, coasters, bowls and flowerpots.

Then came the clothing section: flip-flops and tennis shoes, sweatshirts and jeans, hats and scarves, and then, finally, he reached the open door to the office.

Sylvie stood behind a counter unpacking a box of T-shirts. "Cody!" She put down a handful of shirts and ran to give him a hug.

He put his arms around her and hugged her back. Her topknot tickled his chin and her perfume filled his nostrils. She broke away and looked him up and down. "Heard you were back in town and workin' for the chamber. Glen Thomas." She tsked-tsked. "He's a driver."

"He's okay. Leaves me and Luci pretty much on our own."

Sylvie shook her forefinger. "Yeah. Just don't cross him."

"And that would be how?"

"Forget I said that." She waved a hand, jangling her bracelet made of tiny seashells. Her dangling earrings were also made of shells, and her pink shirt read Willow Beach Rocks. He glanced down at her jeans and flip-flops. Sylvie was a walking advertisement for her souvenir shop.

"Looks like you're doing a great job, taking over for your folks."

"I'm trying. Growing up in the business helps. I've been working here since I was old enough to walk, practically." She grinned. "So what brings you here today? Want me to pose for you?" She placed her hand behind her head and fluttered her eyelashes.

Cody laughed. "Sure. But later. I've a favor to ask first."

"Okay. I'm listening, but let me buy you a drink. C'mon."

She led him to the employee's lounge, which was decorated with orange and red vinyl furniture and a soft drink machine with blinking lights. A few minutes later, bottle of soda in hand and seated on one of the vinyl couches, Cody asked Sylvie to go out to dinner with him and Ben and Luci.

While he talked, she drank her soda and tapped her red fingernails—which matched her toenails—against the bottle.

When he finished, Sylvie set her drink on a glass-topped table. "Let me get this straight. You want me to be your dinner date because you're trying to get this Ben and Luci together, and he needs moral support."

"Something like that."

"And I'm supposed to be your date," she asked.

"Think of it more as friends getting together."

"But you want Ben and Luci to be more than friends? Cody, Cody. Everybody knows Luci's had a crush on you since she was in high school and you were working for the *Herald*."

Cody stiffened. "Maybe so, but now we're just friends."

"Does Luci know that? What are you trying to prove here?"

Cody set down his soda and raised both hands. "I'm not trying to prove anything. Ben says he's interested in Luci, but he's, well, shy, and needs a nudge. I got them talking about birds—Ben's hobby is bird-watching—but I can tell he's a slow mover."

"And what does Luci think about Ben?"

Cody shrugged. "Who knows? Maybe you can find that out. You're not hooked up with anyone right now, are you? I heard you and Eddie Lightner were quits."

Sylvie gave an unladylike snort. "That jerk better not show his face around here again."

"What happened?"

She folded her arms and tilted her head toward the ceiling. "You don't want to know. Anyway, I'm off men right now. Big-time."

"You don't have to worry about me, Sylvie. I'm not looking, either."

"Uh-huh. I don't know, Cody. Don't you think messing around with people's love lives is risky?"

"I think Ben's a good guy and I think Luci's, ah…" Oh, man, he was talking himself into a corner here.

Sylvie gave him a sly look. "You think she's hot."

"Luci is a good friend of mine," he finished in a firm tone. "A friend I want to see happy."

"With another guy. You don't make a bit of sense."

Cody set his jaw. "Hey, it's a free meal."

Sylvie put a finger to her cheek. "Hmm. The Beach Café, you said? I do like their seafood salad."

"Well, there you go."

"I guess I could meet you there."

"Nope. I'll pick you up. We'll make this an official date."

By the time he left, Cody's head hurt. He stood outside a moment and rubbed his temples. If his plan worked, it'd be worth it. Now, all Ben had to do was ask Luci and they'd be set. He'd better not expect Cody to do that, too. The guy had to take some responsibility.

CHAPTER FIVE

"THIS IS A nice evening, isn't it?" Luci said. "The air is extra fresh after the rain we had this morning."

"It is," Ben replied in a monotone. Driving up Main Street seemed to require all his attention.

He looked as neat as a pin, with his hair combed back from his forehead and his jaw clean shaven. He used a strong aftershave, not unpleasant but certainly noticeable. Underneath a lightweight blue windbreaker, he wore his customary formfitting shirt and navy slacks.

She'd debated what to wear herself, finally settling on a dark brown cotton skirt and a T-shirt with a scoop neckline. The butterscotch color set off her red hair, which she'd brushed until it shone.

She wasn't sure what this evening was about. When he'd invited her to dinner, Ben had said it would be a good chance to talk more about the article on birds. But couldn't they do that at the chamber office? Then she'd figured the bird talk was a cover.

Ben had probably seen her around the building and wanted to meet her. When he and Cody were on the fishing trip, Ben must have told Cody of his interest, and Cody said he'd introduce them. That was why Cody had brought Ben to her office that day.

He was nice, if a little stiff and formal. But that was okay. She looked forward to the evening. Maybe if she went out with other men, she could forget about Cody. She still wasn't sure how she felt about him. Was she harboring her teenage crush? Or something more? Spending an evening with Ben might help her to find the answer.

Good thing it wasn't much farther to the Beach Café, because her conversational well was already running dry. At the restaurant, they could talk about the food. And the view. And birds.

AT THE CAFÉ, Marlys, the hostess, greeted them. "Hello, Luci."

"Hi, Marlys, I heard you were working here now."

Marlys nodded. "Now that the twins are in preschool and Joe's on day shift at the plant, I'm back at work. I love it."

Luci introduced Ben.

"Welcome to Willow Beach," Marlys said. "I hope you enjoy the Beach Café. The rest of your group is already seated."

Their group? Before Luci could ask, Marlys picked up a couple menus and motioned them to follow her.

Luci pushed aside her concern and took time to enjoy the restaurant's casual elegance. The place was light and airy with windows on the ocean side and elevated booths on the opposite wall that gave every customer a view. Paintings of nautical scenes decorated the walls.

They hadn't gone far when Luci spotted Cody. It had always been that way. There could be dozens of people around, but if he was in the group, she knew it. And there he was tonight, sitting at one of the window tables. With a woman. Luci stared. His companion was Sylvie Ventura, from the souvenir store.

Was Cody on a date? With Sylvie? A queasy feeling that had nothing to do with hunger invaded Luci's stomach.

She hadn't thought Sylvie would appeal to Cody, but then, what did she know about his taste in women?

More importantly, why was Marlys leading her and Ben to their table?

Not until Cody rose and said, "Hey, you're here," did Luci get it. Cody and Sylvie were the group Marlys had been talking about.

Marlys placed their menus at the two empty seats. "Enjoy your dinner," she said before heading to the front of the restaurant.

Ben pulled out Luci's chair. She remained standing, looking first at Cody and then at Sylvie. "What's going on here?"

"Didn't Ben tell you we were meeting you?" Cody asked.

"Ah, it may have slipped my mind," Ben said, looking sheepish. "But have a seat, Luci."

She dropped into the chair and allowed Ben to scoot her closer to the table.

"So you're Ben," Sylvie said as he sat across from her. "I've been hearing such a lot about you."

Luci frowned at Cody. Whatever was going on here, she'd bet he was behind it.

He met her frown with a grin, and his gaze roved over her. "Looking good tonight, Luci."

"Thanks. You're looking good yourself." She didn't want to think about how good. He'd dressed up for the occasion. A little, anyway. Although he wore his usual jeans, he'd chosen a cream-colored dress shirt instead of a T-shirt. The light color set off his smooth tan and dark hair. Of course, his camera lay on the table beside his place setting.

They studied their menus, but Luci had trouble concentrating. Her mind still churned—along with her stomach—over the shock of Cody and Sylvie.

The waiter appeared, pad and pencil poised to take their orders.

"I'll have the scampi," Sylvie told him.

Cody raised an eyebrow. "What happened to your favorite seafood salad?"

"Didn't want to be the same old boring me tonight." Sylvie batted her eyes in Ben's direction.

"I'm having the salad, boring or not," Luci said. "And knowing you, I bet you're having the seafood fry."

Cody nodded. "Am I predictable, or what?"

Ben opted for the baked halibut. He also

ordered a bottle of wine. When it arrived, he tasted the sample and frowned, tilting his head this way and that. Then he nodded and said, "Yes, very nice."

The waiter smiled a relieved smile and filled their glasses.

That ritual dispensed with, Sylvie leaned across the table and said, "I'm so glad to meet you. I need your help."

Ben frowned as he regarded her over the rim of his wineglass. "You do?"

"Yes. I have the souvenir shop on Main Street, you know, and I ordered these birds—"

"Birds? Live birds?"

"No, no, made of wood. Hand-carved and painted the loveliest colors. But, except for the seagulls, of course, I don't know what kinds of birds they are. And when the customers ask, I don't know what to say. When Cody said you were a bird person, a, ah, what do you call it?"

Ben smiled. "Ornithologist is the term, but 'bird person' will do. Anyway, sure, I'd be glad to help."

Luci was about to say there were any number of books in the library or at the Book Nook that Sylvie could use, not to mention the internet, but sensing Sylvie was on another kind of mission, she kept quiet.

Cody leaned forward. "Luci, remember that little bird you found on the beach that day the *Herald* had their company picnic?"

Luci nodded. "With the broken wing. Poor little thing."

"And we took him to Doc Harper's. And you cried when Doc told you he might not be able to save it."

And you put your arms around me and told me not to worry. But she didn't say that aloud. He probably wouldn't want to be reminded. He probably didn't even remember.

"But he did save it," she said. "So that story has a happy ending."

Ben launched into a tale about a bird they'd saved at the sanctuary where he volunteered. Sylvie listened, her wide-eyed gaze glued to him. Soon he was talking more to her than to the table at large, and when he and she discovered they both liked the old Alfred Hitchcock movie *The Birds*, that led to a discussion of other old movies.

Their meals arrived. Luci concentrated on her salad, which was as good as she remembered, loaded with fresh shrimp and crabmeat and chunks of salmon. Cody dug into his seafood fry, although he still attempted to get a word in when either Sylvie or Ben stopped talking long enough to take a bite of their food.

Later, over crème brûlée, Sylvie and Ben were still talking only to each other. The conversation had moved from old movies to, of all things, sword fighting. Luci sipped her coffee and gazed at the dunes, where the grass waved rhythmically in the wind. Beyond the beach was the ocean, where an orange sun dipped low over calm waters.

Cody was looking out the window, too, and fingering his camera. He caught her eye. She looked pointedly at the camera and then back at him. They both smiled.

Luci sighed. She knew Cody well. Too well.

When there was finally a lull in Sylvie and Ben's conversation, Cody said, "How about a walk on the new boardwalk?"

Sylvie blinked at Cody and then at Luci, as though suddenly reminded of their presence. "That's a good idea. I love the new boardwalk."

"Ever been to Atlantic City's boardwalk?"

Ben folded his napkin and laid it beside his plate.

"Why, no," Sylvie said. "You'll have to tell me all about it."

Ben's account of the famed landmark led them all the way outside and down the path to the beach. Luci marveled at Ben. After barely speaking to her on the way to the restaurant, his words spewed forth, as though a dam had broken. He was eloquent, too. And gesturing, as if he were onstage. She guessed he was, playing to an audience of one.

They reached the boardwalk and climbed the ramp. As they began their stroll, Luci buttoned her jacket against the stiff breeze. She was glad she'd worn flats and marveled that Sylvie could walk in her high-heeled sandals.

Pointing to a mounted telescope, Sylvie sped up into a trot. "Oh, let's look," she called over her shoulder.

Ben took off after her.

"Don't you want to look, too?" Luci asked Cody.

"I've got my scope right here." He patted his camera.

Sylvie and Ben reached the scope. He dug into his pocket, pulled out some coins and stuck them into the slot. Sylvie bent to look in the eyepiece. He stood behind her, putting his arms around her to grasp the scope and turn it from side to side.

Cody raised his camera and aimed it at Ben and Sylvie.

Sylvie spotted him. "Oh, there goes Mr. Cameraman."

"Look through the scope again, Sylvie," Cody said. "There, that's it. Now, Ben, lean over again, like you're showing her how to use it."

"He is," Sylvie said.

Luci rolled her eyes.

Finished with the scope, Sylvie and Ben stood at the railing with the setting sun as a backdrop, and Cody took their picture.

"Okay," Cody said, "now, Ben, I want one of you and Luci."

"Me and Ben?" Luci asked.

"Yes, ah, at the railing, too, but, let's see, looking at each other. Silhouettes of your profiles against the sunset. Yes, that'd be good."

Luci stood at the railing and turned to Ben. He faced her, too, but instead of looking into her eyes, his gaze drifted over her shoulder.

Standing nearby, Sylvie folded her arms and tapped her foot.

Cody continued his picture taking. By the time they'd reached the end of the boardwalk and were turning around to head back, the sun had set and the water had turned a deep turquoise. Ben was beside Luci again, and Cody walked with Sylvie. Nobody said more than a few words, and when they reached Cody's SUV and Ben's truck, their goodbyes were brief and polite.

On the drive home, Luci thought about trying to make conversation, but, in truth, she didn't have the energy. Ben lapsed into his characteristic silence. No, not characteristic. Sylvie had pushed a button and, like a mechanical doll, Ben had come to life.

"Thanks for dinner and the nice evening," she said when they reached her apartment.

"You're welcome. I'll walk you to your door," he added but made no move to silence the truck's engine.

"No need. It's right there."

"Okay. Good night, then. When you want to talk more about birds, give me a call."

"I most certainly will."

"So what was that all about, Sylvie?"

"What was what all about?"

He took his gaze from the road long enough to meet her innocent eyes with a glare. "You know what I'm talking about. You were flirting with Ben."

She pressed her lips together and fingered her purse, which was balanced on her lap. "I couldn't help it. I took one look at him and our eyes met and, well, I just knew that he was special."

"I thought you'd sworn off men. After Eddie gave you such a bad time."

"I thought I had, too, but, well, our eyes met and—"

"You already said that."

She shrugged. "There's not much more to say."

Cody set his jaw. He'd wanted to help Ben and Luci, directing the conversation, seeing that they got to know each other better. And Sylvie? Well, she was along for...for the sea-food salad, like she'd agreed. Only she hadn't fulfilled her end of the bargain.

"You should know better than to try manipulating people," Sylvie said.

"I wasn't manipulating, I was, ah, assisting, guiding, mentoring."

"Manipulating," she said, more emphatic than before.

He slowed the SUV to turn off Main Street, heading for Sylvie's house. "So what now?"

She shrugged. "What do you mean?"

"Did he ask to see you again?"

"As if that's any of your business."

"I think it is. I'm the one who got you into this."

Sylvie heaved a deep sigh. "Okay, no, he did not. But he will." She nodded, setting her topknot in motion.

Cody snorted. "How do you know that?"

"A woman just knows, that's all."

"Are men really that transparent?"

Sylvie grasped her purse, lifted it and plunked it down on her lap again. "I'd better shut up, before I give away too many secrets of the sisterhood."

Cody shut up, too, and they rode on in silence.

They reached her house, which was enclosed by a rickety fence strung with fishnets, colorful buoys and pieces of driftwood.

The yard was a mixture of sand and crushed seashells, with tufts of grass sprouting here and there.

She opened the gate and led them up the path to the front door. A wind chime made of seashells hanging next to the door clacked in the light breeze.

"Thanks, Cody." Sylvie stood on tiptoe and kissed his cheek.

"You're welcome—I think."

She turned to slip her key in the lock but then stopped and faced him again. "Oh, I almost forgot. Can I have one of those pictures you took of Ben and me tonight? I want to put it on my Facebook page, to let Eddie know I've moved on."

"Sure, but you just said Ben didn't ask to see you again."

"He will," she said and smiled. "He will."

"WHAT CAN I help you with, Mom?" Luci asked. After a stressful week at work and the so-called date with Ben Shapiro last night, she looked forward to a relaxing Sunday with her family.

Anna stood at the island in the spacious kitchen, slicing a head of lettuce on the chopping board. She pushed a lock of hair from her forehead with the back of one hand. "Hello, honey. You can work on this salad while I baste the roast."

Luci sniffed the air. "It smells wonderful." Picking up the knife where her mother had laid it, she sliced the lettuce while Anna crossed the room to the stove.

The children's voices drifted in from the screened-in porch adjacent to the dining room. "Sounds like the kids are having a good time," Luci began, but just then a scream rent the air. "Uh-oh, somebody's not happy."

Anna closed the oven door and straightened. "That sounds like Megan. She has trouble getting along with the older kids, sometimes."

Arliss entered the kitchen, holding a tearful Megan by the hand. "Maybe Grandma can find something you can help with," Arliss was saying. "Oh, hi, Luci. How was your date last night?"

Luci's mouth dropped open. "How'd you know about that?"

"You forget Don and Cody are buddies?" Anna handed Megan a stack of paper napkins. "Here, darlin', put one of these at each place at the table. Okay?"

Megan pouted, but she nodded, took the napkins and trotted off to the dining room.

"Buddies, humph," Luci said. "More like gossips."

"So how was it?" Arliss lifted a pot of potatoes from the stove and moved to the sink to pour off the water.

"It was…okay."

"You like Ben?"

"He was nice." She looked around. "Where's Fran?" Usually the four of them worked together in the kitchen.

Arliss set down the pot and gave a dismissive wave. "Oh, she's on her phone. Big open house today in Oceanside."

"The agency is certainly keeping her busy, aren't they?" Luci scooped the lettuce into a salad bowl.

"I guess for her, selling houses beats staying home with the kids."

"Good thing she has you to take care of them," Luci said.

"I don't mind. I really do love kids," Arliss said.

Finished with the salad, Luci stepped onto

the porch to call the others for dinner. The three older children were playing a board game on the tile floor. Francine sat by herself in a corner, cell phone glued to her ear. She and Luci exchanged waves. Luci expected to find the men watching TV, but today only Will and Don were in front of the set. "Time to eat." She looked around. "Where's Dad?"

"He went outside." Don motioned toward the sliding glass door.

While he and Will corralled the children and headed for the dining room, Luci opened the door and stepped outside. The usual brisk breeze blew off the ocean. She walked along the stone path that bordered the lawn. Erv was nowhere in sight. Then she spotted him standing at the edge of the property, gazing at the ocean.

She came up behind him. "Dad."

He gave a start and turned. "Oh, Luci. Hi."

His eyes looked tired, and there were lines around his mouth she'd never noticed before.

"Didn't mean to startle you. What are you doing out here all by yourself? Are you okay?"

"Sure. Just needed some fresh air." He

raised his arm, and she stepped under it for a hug. "How's my Luci?"

"I'm fine, but hungry. Let's go eat."

DINNER WAS USUALLY a noisy affair, with lots of talk and laughter. Today, except for the kids' chatter, everyone was sober and quiet. Her father, who often shared stories about the bank or his golf game, said little. Will, who worked for a boat dealer at the marina, exchanged a few words with Don about boats for sale. Arliss and Anna talked awhile about a dress Arliss was making for Hannah. Francine kept glancing at her text messages and left the table twice to take phone calls. When she came back from the second call, she pushed in her chair instead of sitting down.

"I have to go," she said. "Sandy has to leave early, and I need to take over the open house."

Will frowned and folded his arms. "I figured that would happen. Sandy's a flake. Okay, we'll see you when we see you."

Fran opened her mouth to reply but then snapped it shut. She gave Anna a kiss on the cheek, waved at the others and was gone.

After dinner, they usually gathered on the

sunporch to watch a movie or play cards or a board game. Luci took out a deck from the cupboard. "Who's for fifty-cent rummy?" she said, shuffling the cards. "Don, you won last time, so we're out to get you."

"I can't stay." Don hovered near the door.

Luci stopped shuffling. "What? Why?"

"I told Ole Swenson I'd look at his boat. It's up for sale."

"But that's a charter boat. Why would you want to buy that?"

"We're just talkin'."

Don cast a furtive look at Erv, but Erv was gazing out at the yard.

Megan started to cry at something her sister said, and Will decided they'd better go home. Erv mumbled something about having work to do in his study. Arliss, Luci and Anna cleaned up the kitchen, but as soon as they were finished, Arliss and the children left.

Luci hung up the last of the dish towels and then turned to her mother. "What's wrong with everybody today?"

"What do you mean, dear?"

"This certainly wasn't one of our usual Sunday dinners, and not at all what I'd hoped for my first Sunday back in town. I was looking forward to us all having a good time visiting, playing games, watching TV, like we always do."

"We've had our off days before," Anna said, patting her shoulder. "Disagreements and discord happen to the best of families."

Despite her mother's attempt to reassure her, Luci still worried. Were they all having an *off day*? Or was something more serious wrong?

CHAPTER SIX

THE FOLLOWING MONDAY, Luci sat at her desk in the chamber office, sorting through the information she'd gathered for the sand-castle contest. She'd been working hard to come up with something that, as Glen had said, would make the chamber of commerce look good.

"Hey, Luci."

She sighed and then squared her shoulders.

Cody rounded her desk and stood in front of her. "Good morning."

"Morning, Cody, just the man I want to see. I've been working on the sand-castle contest." She tapped the stack of papers on her desk. "I have some ideas I want to run by you."

"Something for me and my trusty camera, I hope." He patted his camera slung around his neck.

"Of course. That's why you were hired."

"True enough."

"Have a seat and let's get to it." She gestured to the worktable, most of which was still piled high with all the material she had to sort through.

She walked over and sat, expecting him to follow. He didn't, and when she turned to see why, he was frowning and rubbing his jaw. "What?" she said.

"I need to clear the air first—about Saturday night."

Luci tensed. "What's to discuss? Your plan bombed. I'd think you'd want to sweep that failure under the rug."

He spread his hands. "Now, wait a minute. What do you mean, 'my plan'?"

She folded her arms. "I think you know."

"Let's start at the beginning. Have you heard from Ben?"

"I have. He called early this morning to say he was emailing me an article on the bird refuge he thought I'd be interested in. And he did. Want to see it?" She stood and took a step toward her desk.

He shook his head. "Not now." He paced to the window and then turned slightly and gave her a sideways look. "He didn't say anything about our dinner the other night?"

"No. Why should he?"

Cody shrugged. "I don't know. Just asking."

She let a couple seconds go by and then said, "Sylvie called me last night, though."

Cody narrowed his eyes. "What'd she want?"

"Oh, just to talk." Luci hid a smile, enjoying watching Cody squirm. Served him right.

"What about? Or is it sacred women-talk?"

"Nothing sacred. She wanted to apologize. For 'stealing Ben away.' I assured her she hadn't. He was a new acquaintance, not someone I was involved with. I told her I didn't really know why he'd asked me to dinner."

Cody was looking out the window again. Or pretending to. She went to stand beside him. In the courtyard, several employees from another office drank coffee and ate sandwiches at one of the wrought-iron tables. In another corner, a gardener pulled a rake through a patch of grass. Cody fingered his camera, and she thought he was going to take a picture, but the gesture seemed to be more a preoccupation than a signal of intent.

"So, do you?" she asked.

He kept staring out the window. "Do I what?"

"Know why he asked me to dinner."

"Okay, here's the story. He asked me about your situation."

"My situation."

"Yeah, you know." He waved a hand. "Were you seeing anyone. Were you available."

"Available. Like an apartment for rent."

"Aw, come on, Luci, you know what I mean. He wanted to know if you're dating anyone."

She covered her mouth to suppress a giggle. She was so enjoying this. "And you said?"

"Not that I know of." He slanted her a glance. "You aren't, are you?"

Was that a worried note in his voice? She studied her fingernails and said, "Not at the moment."

"I didn't think so."

"Am I really so predictable?"

"No, no, of course not. Anyway, he said he wanted to ask you to dinner. Dinner was his idea." He stepped back and raised his hands. "That's the truth, I swear."

"Okay, okay, I believe you."

Cody clasped his hands behind his back and paced. "But, being the shy guy he is, or that I thought he was, he wanted me to come, too. I needed a date, so I asked Sylvie. That was the setup."

Luci let that sink in while the people outside tossed their coffee cups and plates into a nearby trash can and headed for the door. The gardener moved on to another patch of grass.

"Okay," Luci said, "but if you're interested in her, you're out of luck, because she's seeing Ben."

"Really? So he did ask her out?"

She knit her brows. "Why does that surprise you?"

He shrugged. "I guess it doesn't."

"Anyway, she wanted to apologize for coming on so strong at dinner. I told her not to worry. It happens that way, sometimes."

"It does?"

Luci stuck her hands on her hips and shook her head. "Honestly, Cody, sometimes you're so clueless, I wonder about you."

Cody stepped back. "Hey, I've got other things on my mind."

"I guess you do. Anyway, I told her I had

no claim on Ben and no interest in him other than exchanging information about birds."

"I'm glad you got that squared away with Sylvie, but shouldn't Ben have something to say about it?"

"Oh, I think he spoke loud and clear the other night, don't you? Or didn't you notice?"

"I noticed. I'm not that clueless. They were all over each other."

"It was kinda funny, really." She giggled.

Cody chuckled, and then they were both laughing.

"What's going on here?"

Glen's sharp tone brought Luci to her senses. Her laughter died away. Their boss stood in the doorway, hands on his hips, a frown on his face.

"We're, ah, telling funny stories," she said.

Glen raised his eyebrows and said nothing.

"About, ah, something that happened the other night."

"What's so funny about it?" Glen asked.

"You had to be there," Cody said.

"Oh." Glen made a dismissive wave. "Well, keep it down. We've having a meeting next door."

"We will," Luci promised.

When he'd left, Cody pressed his lips together and shook his head. "I don't think he ever has a good time, do you?"

"Not that I've seen. He's the boss, though, so we'd better do what he says. Just one last thing."

"What's that?"

"No more fixing me up with dates. I will do my own fixing, thank you."

"But I didn't—"

Luci held up a hand. "I'm not going to argue with you. I'm just telling you how I feel. If you truly are my friend, you'll honor my request. Now, let's talk about the sand-castle contest."

"ACCORDING TO THE MAP, this entire stretch of beach will be used for the contest." Cody held out the map and waited for Luci to finish entering something on her tablet.

They'd decided to walk to the beach and inspect the area where the contest would take place. He hoped this project would go more smoothly than their trip to the cranberry farm. He liked her ideas, but he needed to have some freedom to be creative, too.

Luci closed the gap between them and

studied the map. "Yes, the contest has grown. When I used to take part with Don and Francine, there were a dozen entrants at most. Now, there must be a hundred or more, lined up and down the beach."

"That'll be a lot of pictures to take."

"You'll love it," she said, rolling her eyes, "because that's what you do."

"Of course. And Glen will be happy, too."

"I hope so," she said. "I haven't told him yet. I wanted to run the idea by you first and make sure we worked out all the kinks."

This year, in addition to the usual cash prizes and medals given to the winners, the chamber would present all the contestants with photos of themselves building their sand castles. Cody would take the pictures, of course, and they'd be processed and printed on-site so people could claim them when the day was over. The photos would be a gesture of goodwill on the part of the chamber of commerce.

Luci continued to study the map, tracing the route with her forefinger and then looking at the beach. The wind picked up strands of her red hair that had escaped the knot at her nape. She wrinkled her nose in the cute way she had when deep in thought. Automatically, Cody brought his camera up and snapped a couple shots.

She looked around and frowned. "Cody, will you stop, please? And focus."

"I am focusing," he said. "On you. Couldn't resist."

"Forget me and keep your attention on what we're doing here. Please. Come on, let's go look at the spot where we'll set up our tent."

Following the map, they trudged along the sand, working their way toward the dunes. A few clouds drifted across the sky, and the air was cooler than usual for June. Farther down the beach, where driving on the hard-packed sand was allowed, a few cars rolled past, dodging the waves. He used to do that, too, when he was in high school, and even on visits home from college.

Cody missed those carefree days. And, although he was happy as a freelancer, his determination to follow his dream had taken away some of his freedom to be spontaneous. He glanced at Luci. What would happen, he wondered, if they chucked their map, climbed into his SUV and started driving with no particular destination in mind? No cares, no worries, no big, lofty goals, just taking each day as it came and seeing what happened.

Crazy thought. She was a nester, like her brother had said. She'd put down deep roots here in Willow Beach.

"Our tent will be here." Luci's voice jolted his thoughts back to the present. They'd reached the dunes, and she pointed to a spot that corresponded to one on the map. "The food vendors' carts will be on the other side of us, and over there will be the bandstand."

Cody forced himself to focus. "Looks good to me."

"The chamber will set up generators so we can run our equipment."

"Sounds as though you've arranged for everything."

"Except the folders for the photos. We need to see Brooke Anderson at the Blue Gull Gallery about those. She said to come in today. They've agreed to donate the folders if their logo appears on the back." She frowned. "You are available to go with me, aren't you?"

"Of course. I'm on the job."

"Okay, just thought you might be getting

bored or restless and need to take off for, oh, I don't know." She shrugged.

"Timbuktu? It's on my list. But not today. Today, I'm yours for as long as you need me. So, lead on to the Blue Gull."

At the art gallery, Brooke was busy with a customer, so Luci motioned Cody to the back of the store where the art supplies were kept. On the way, he looked at the displays, impressed with the various ways artists expressed themselves. Especially eye-catching were driftwood carvings arranged on glass shelves. Another area featured oil paintings of sailboats with colorful spinnakers. Even some of the handmade jewelry caught his eye, silver and gold necklaces and earrings set with turquoise and other stones of various shapes, sizes and colors.

He and Luci were looking through bins of matted prints when Brooke found them.

"Hey," she said, a smile lighting her face. "Two of my favorite people."

"Your gallery looks good," Cody said.

Brooke's smile widened at the compliment. "Thanks. Luci, did you see the tie-dyed tops?" She pointed to a rack of bright-colored clothing. "A woman in Oceanside makes them."

"I did," Luci said. "I'll come in and try some on when I have more time. Right now, we need folders for the sand-castle-contest photos."

"Sure. Let's take a look at what we have."

She led them to a bin of precut mats and folders. Shuffling through the folders, she pulled out several and laid them side by side on a nearby table. "This style would be perfect." She pointed to one. "It has a backing that will secure the photo and it comes in various colors. We can have them printed with both the chamber logo and ours."

Luci picked up the folder and inspected it. "Looks good to me." She turned to Cody. "What do you think?"

Cody nodded. "I'd say perfect."

"Super," Brooke said. "Come on over to the counter, and I'll write up a proposal that you can show Glen."

Cody kept browsing while Brooke entered their order into the computer. "You've done a lot with this place. It used to be smaller."

Brooke nodded. "When the ice-cream shop next door moved, Stan and I bought that space and knocked out the wall in between. That really opened up the gallery."

"You found your niche here," Luci said.

"I did," Brooke replied. "And it looks like you've found yours, Luci. Your dream job at the chamber, right?"

"Yes. Some of my friends who graduated when I did are out there scrambling for jobs, and I didn't even have to go looking."

Brooke tapped the keyboard and lifted her chin as she focused on the screen. "It helps to have connections."

"What do you mean?" Luci wrinkled her brow.

Brooke's hands stilled. "Why, just that with your dad and Glen being such good friends, I'm sure Erv put in a good word for you. What's wrong with that?"

"I'd like to think I got the job because I'm qualified," Luci said.

Her tone prompted Cody to jump in. "Very qualified. I can attest to that."

Luci turned her frown on him, and he sent her a smile in return, hoping she'd get the message that he was only trying to help—and that he really meant what he'd said.

"I'm sure you are qualified," Brooke said smoothly. She pressed a key and the printer chugged. When the paper rolled out, she plucked it from the tray and held it out to Luci. "Here's a summary of what we discussed. Let me know when you get Glen's okay."

Out on the sidewalk, Luci marched alongside Cody in silence. When they stopped at the corner for a red light, he turned to her. "You still upset? Like Brooke said, nothing wrong with having connections."

"So you agree with her? That I got the job because of my father's friendship with Glen Thomas?"

"I don't know that. I don't have the facts."

"But that's what everyone thinks, isn't it?"

"Luci, how would I know what everyone in town thinks? I haven't been around much for the last few years. And so what if they do? Can't you be qualified and have connections?"

Luci stuck out her chin. "I just don't want people to think I got the job because of my father's influence."

The light changed and they crossed the street. They walked awhile in silence, dodging people coming toward them and stopping at the next corner when they missed the light again. Cody looked at the gray sky. Was the sun going to show today or not?

Luci sighed. The set of her jaw told him she was still in a funk. He grasped her elbow as they stepped off the curb. "Come on, let's hit Charlie's. You'll feel better after some food."

Over lunch, he steered the conversation in a new direction, hoping to bring back at least some of her earlier enthusiasm. "What's next on our agenda?" he asked. "As I recall, we've got a lot of work to do."

"I know. I'm just beginning to tackle the brochures that need updating. Did you notice the one on the lighthouse? Since it was published, the light keeper's quarters have been remodeled and the gift shop has been expanded." She looked wistful. "I remember when I was an intern at the *Herald* and they did a feature on the lighthouse. Eva Townson—she was Eva Sinclair then—took me along on one of her interviews. That was fun."

"Yeah, working for the *Herald* was good times. But now you're in charge. Isn't that something?"

"I guess." She sighed.

"Okay, we'll hit the lighthouse. What else?"

"The resort at Pine Lake, the wildlife refuge—"

"Now, that's a place where I could be very busy."

By the time they had finished lunch and were on their way to the office, she was smiling again. And so was the sun, which had finally broken out from the clouds.

When they reached the chamber, Cody stopped at the door. "If you don't need me anymore today, I think I'll head out."

"Out? You're leaving town?"

"Not any farther than Oceanside. There's a camera shop that I want to check out."

"Oh. Okay. Thanks for your help today—and thanks for the cheer up."

"I have got no idea what you're talking about."

"Uh-huh. I know you were trying to make me feel better."

He grinned. "Am I that transparent?"

"Sometimes."

"So, did it work?"

She bit her lip for a moment and then said softly, "Yeah, it did."

She gazed up at him, her hazel eyes wide, her lips slightly parted. His chest tightened, and he was seized by the urge to take her in his arms and kiss her. He gave himself a shake. That would be a crazy thing to do, out here in public, in the middle of the day. That would be crazy, period.

"Don't forget the chamber meeting on Thursday," she said. "Twelve o'clock."

He came down to earth with a jolt. "Say what?"

"The monthly meeting of the outfit we work for?" She tilted her head and eyed him. "Cody, are you okay?"

"Yeah, sure. Just drifted for a couple seconds. But, all right, the chamber meeting. Think I'll skip it and drive up the coast. There should be some interesting tide pools."

"But Glen expects us both to be there."

"I'm just the summer help, Luci. This isn't my dream job."

"Cody! I need your support."

He held up both hands. "All right, all right. See you then."

She smiled, looking kissable again. He'd better get out of there quickly. With a wave, he turned and hurried down the hall.

As Luci watched Cody disappear around the corner, she ran her fingers over her lips. She could swear he'd been about to kiss her. Not a good idea, especially at the door to her office. And so, she'd blurted a reminder of the upcoming meeting.

Maybe she'd only imagined that he was about to kiss her.

No, a woman knows those things. She just knows.

A part of her wanted the kiss. But she knew nothing could ever come of it. Just like a bud became a flower, a kiss could blossom into love. But that would never happen between her and Cody. She was staying here in Willow Beach and, come the end of summer, he was moving on.

Walking through the reception area, Luci glimpsed Marge bent over the file cabinets in the adjacent workroom. The door to Glen's office was open, but he was nowhere to be seen. She would have to present her plans for the sand-castle contest another time.

When she walked into her office, the pile of papers was waiting for her on the worktable. Luci checked her wristwatch. Barely one thirty. She still had lots of time to sort through some of the file folders. She'd keep an ear out for Glen's arrival—not hard to do, given his booming voice—and when he came in, she'd present her proposal.

She'd no more than taken the first folder from the stack when Marge bustled in, her arms loaded with papers, magazines and folders. She stopped short of the table and twisted her lips as though she'd just eaten a lemon.

"I hate to do this to you," Marge said. "But I'm still cleaning out the workroom. Boss's orders."

Inwardly, Luci groaned. Then she grinned and beckoned Marge forward. "Bring it on, Marge. Bring it on."

CHAPTER SEVEN

LATER THAT AFTERNOON, Cody left Hall's Camera Store in Oceanside with his new lens tucked in his jacket pocket. He'd spent over an hour in the store, losing track of time as he browsed the equipment. Now he craved a cup of coffee.

He saw a Starbucks and a Tully's, either of which would ordinarily suit him, but on the way into town, he'd glimpsed a little café that looked interesting. Might even give him a chance to try out his new lens.

Five minutes later, he pulled into the parking lot of Mac's Café. Above the door was a neon sign in the shape of a coffee cup with steam curling from it. A picture of a cinnamon roll dripping with icing was in the window. The caption read, Mmm, Good! He grinned. This was his kind of place, all right.

Inside, the aroma of brewing coffee mingled with the sugary smell of pastries, which were enclosed in a display case. Tables filled the center of the room, with a counter and the kitchen on one side and large, private booths on the other. He slipped into an empty booth, and a waitress came and took his order. When his food arrived, he sipped the coffee and dug into the cinnamon roll that was indeed "mmm, good."

He was about to unwrap his new lens when his phone dinged with a text message. He smiled when he saw the sender was Dexter Hunter. Cody and Dex and Shar Williams had been on several assignments together, the most recent being Mexico.

Hey out there in nowhereville. c u soon

What? They were coming to Willow Beach? He'd invited them, but they'd wanted to spend the summer with their families—Shar's in Omaha and Dex's in Denver.

He wrote back: When?

The answer came: Probly Aug. More later.

Cody tucked his phone away and took out his new lens. He'd be happy to see Dex and Shar again. They were lots of laughs but serious about their work. Sometimes, the three of them competed with one another as they elbowed their way through a crowd searching for the best shots. But they always ended up friends.

Luci's image popped into his mind, and for a second he saw both of them traipsing off on one of his trips. Yeah, like that would work. They were as mismatched as…as… While he sat there trying to think of something, he became aware of voices drifting over the top of the booth behind him.

A woman said, "I didn't want to upset you."

"Upset me?" a man answered. "How could you not? I…I can't believe this."

"No reason to lie."

The man spoke again, but his voice had dropped and the words were unintelligible. The woman replied, and the man said, "…our town…my family…"

"If you'd just…"

By that time, Cody was fairly certain he knew the man's identity. Even so, he really didn't want to eavesdrop. Whatever was happening in that booth was none of his business. He was about to pick up his check and head for the cash register when the woman said, "Need to go… Mavis is waiting."

The woman slid from the booth and passed by Cody on her way to the front door. Cody ducked his head and pretended to be absorbed in his new lens.

She was small, probably no more than five foot five. The woman wore jeans and a short-sleeved pink blouse and had gray hair pulled into a thick ponytail. She had a slight limp and walked with a cane.

"I'll be there…" the man said. "On my way." He plunked change onto the table, rose out of the booth and walked by, head down.

Yep, Cody was right: the man was Luci's father, Ervin Monroe.

Before Cody had time to look down again, Ervin mumbled something, swung around and headed back to his booth. His face was as pale as his white shirt, and his gray hair stood on end, as though he'd been running his fingers through it.

He was still mumbling when his gaze landed on Cody. He stopped and stared.

"Cody!"

"Hey, Erv." Cody gave a little salute.

"What're you doing here?" Erv asked, his

tone sharp. "Aren't you supposed to be working with Luci?"

"I'm done for the day. I've been at the camera shop in the mall. New lens." He held up the lens.

"Oh. Well, good for you." As if anticipating a similar question from Cody, he said, "I, uh, client meeting." He nodded toward the front of the café, where the woman waited. Even from a distance, Cody could see that her eyes were red, as though she'd been crying.

"Forgot my check." Erv reached around to the other booth and snatched the slip of paper from the table. "Well, ah, carry on."

"You, too."

Cody took out a lens cloth and vigorously polished his new lens. Once he heard the front door close, he looked out the window to see if the two were still together. They were. Erv was talking and waving his arms, and the woman had her head bowed as they walked down the sidewalk. Then they were lost from view.

A client meeting? He seriously doubted that. He'd seen Erv in his office at the bank, sitting like a king in his high-backed leather

chair, his elbows propped on the chair's arms
and his hands making a tent with the fingers touching. There, he'd looked severe and,
above all, professional, not pasty faced and
his hair tousled. This was something else. He
couldn't help wondering what.

Wait a minute. What Ervin Monroe did
was no business of his.

Except maybe where Luci was concerned.

Luci thought her family was perfect. She
would be more than upset if she found out her
father was…was what? He didn't know the
facts, so until he did, he'd better keep quiet.

"WHERE DO YOU want these lamps, Mom?"

Olive looked up from arranging a group
of porcelain figurines on one of the shelves
built into a wall. "Put them on the tables at either end of these shelves. They're good reading lamps."

They were conducting what Cody called
"new-house day." Every few months Olive
brought furnishings and knickknacks
home from her shop, the Antique Attic, and
swapped them with items she then took to the
store. "Keeps both places fresh," she'd said.

"And I don't get bored looking at the same decor all the time."

Cody never stayed in one place long enough to get bored with the decor. As far as his apartment was concerned, he liked having everything in a certain spot, permanently. Cameras had their own spots, and boxes and bins were all but cemented in their places. He had to know where his equipment was so he could easily grab and go.

Cody picked up one of the lamps and carried it to the end table by an easy chair upholstered in rose-colored cloth. On the other end of the shelves sat an identical pairing of end table and chair.

"The pink roses on the lamps match the chairs," he observed, positioning the lamp on the table and then kneeling to plug in the cord.

"I love those lamps. Your father gave them to me, and I would never sell them."

"Dad picked these out?" Cody went to get the other lamp.

"He did. I've always liked flowers—you know that—and he saw them in Low's Furniture Store and bought them for my birthday. They didn't go with anything we had then, but I put them front and center in our living room and I've always kept them because he gave them to me."

Her voice cracked on the last words. Cody put down the lamp and gave his mom a hug. "You and Dad had a great relationship."

"We did. And all too short."

"Why didn't you ever marry again?"

"I don't know," she said.

"What happened to that guy who used to walk his dog by our house? Mel something. The dog was a cocker spaniel, who sat up and begged for treats."

"Mel Simpson. He was visiting his daughter, who lives a couple blocks from here. The dog was hers."

"So what happened to Mel?"

"He went back to Wenatchee a couple years ago."

"You never heard from him again? I thought he kinda liked you."

"Oh, yes. We email and talk on the phone. But we're just friends. His wife had passed away, and he said he wasn't ready to, you know, move on."

"You can understand that, having lost Dad."

"Yes, I know what Mel was going through."

"It's great you and Dad were so happy, though."

She sighed. "At least I had him for a while. But now I have you. And I'm very thankful for that."

"Me, too, Mom. I'll always be here for you."

He gave her shoulders another squeeze and then let go. She returned to her figurines, alternating them with groups of books, and he picked up a throw rug from a pile stacked against one wall. "In front of the sofa with this, right?"

She glanced over her shoulder. "Yes, let's try it there."

"Speaking of happy couples… Erv and Anna are still going strong, don't you think?" He cast her a sideways glance, hoping she wouldn't think his question odd.

She slid another handful of books onto the shelves. "Oh, yes. The only thing I've heard her complain about is that Erv sometimes drives the kids too hard. He's always had high expectations for them."

"Mmm. But they're a solid couple?"

"They are." She stopped and wrinkled her

brow. "I did hear rumors of a time they were separated…"

His ears perked up. "What's that?"

"They took some time apart. But not for very long. That was before we moved here, and I don't know the details. Anna never speaks of it, but I heard about it from Mabel Murray. You know what a gossip she is. Why are you asking?"

Before he could make up an answer, she tossed him a sly smile. "Oh, I know—because of Luci."

"Luci? I'm not getting the connection here."

"Well, if Luci comes from a happy family, chances are she'll be able to make a happy family herself."

"Huh?"

"You're finally thinking of settling down. Good. I've been worried about you."

"Me and Luci?" His chest had tightened up all of a sudden. "Why does everyone think Luci and I are destined to be a couple, when nothing could be further from the truth? Even if I were looking, she would not be on my radar. She's the kid who had a crush on me when she was in high school."

Olive stepped back and raised both hands. "Whoa. Did I hit a nerve?"

"No, you did not."

"Well, think about it. She's not in high school anymore. And in case you hadn't noticed, she's a mature woman now—and a very attractive one at that. Plus being nice and smart."

"We're friends, that's all. That's all we'll ever be."

He was about to tell her about fixing up Luci and Ben, but before he could get the words out, she said, "You didn't really want her and that new man in town—Ben what's-his-name—to get together, did you?"

"What? How did you know— I mean, asking her out was his idea—"

She laughed. "You ought to know there are very few secrets in Willow Beach. Everyone knows everyone's business."

"Which is exactly why I don't want to live here permanently." He made some grumbling noises and then added, "I like my privacy. And I wasn't fixing them up."

Olive tilted her head and eyed him.

Uncomfortable under her all-too-familiar scrutiny, he said, "Okay, so maybe I was hoping. Luci's a good kid. I like her. I want to see her happy."

"With someone else."

"Of course, with someone else," he fumed. "Look, can we drop the subject?" He propped his hands on his hips and looked around, his gaze landing on the rugs still rolled up by the wall. "Where do you want the other rugs?"

"Hmm, let's see. The green one in front of the fireplace and the purple in the guest bedroom. And then we're quitting because it's time for me to hustle up some dinner."

When she pushed a lock of hair from her forehead, he noticed her eyes looked tired and her smile a bit forced. A lump formed in his throat. He went over and hugged her again. "Let me take you out for dinner tonight. We'll celebrate."

"Celebrate what?"

"Oh, I don't know. How about your being the best mom ever?"

She laughed and then kissed him on the cheek. "I'd like that," she said. "I'd like that very much."

"So, WHAT DO you think, Mr., ah, Glen?"

"Hmm." Glen rubbed his chin as he studied the photo folder. "I'm not quite getting how this draws attention to the chamber of commerce."

"Well, besides the chamber logo on the back of the folder—" she turned it over and pointed to the logo "—each contestant will receive a packet of coupons from the members' businesses. It's the same packet that goes into the basket we give to new residents. That makes two perks for entering the contest—besides a chance to win the prize money and a medal. Pretty good deal, I'd say."

"Let me see here." He picked up the order form from the Blue Gull Gallery. While he perused it, Luci sat back and took a deep breath. She'd hoped Glen would take to her idea right away.

Watching his face made her nervous, so she looked around his office instead. His desk was a huge kidney-shaped piece of metal so shiny you could see your reflection in it. The only items on the desk were an in-and-out basket, a pen and a small calendar. Behind his desk was a long table that had all his electronic equipment. He had the same big windows facing the courtyard that her office had, except instead of a worktable, his space had several easy chairs clustered around a coffee table. The walls were filled with pictures of Glen with various people. She recognized the mayor, an actor and a golf pro.

He cleared his throat, capturing her attention. "Well, Luci…" He tapped the order form with his forefinger. "If this is your best—"

Her best? Of course it was. And what was wrong with the idea, anyway? Everyone else thought it was great.

"—we'll give it a try."

"What exactly does that mean?"

He looked at her over the top of his glasses. "It means you can tell Brooke at the Blue Gull to go ahead and order the folders."

"I'll get back to her right away."

"And you handle all the details. This is your baby. Make us look good."

WHERE WAS CODY? Would he show up for the chamber meeting? Maybe he'd decided to go chase the tide pools, after all.

Staff from the Beach Café were busy putting the finishing touches on the buffet lunch, and all sorts of enticing aromas floated through the air.

Tables filled the room, with the head table at one end. The members were greeting one another and networking. Luci knew most of them, except for those who'd established businesses while she'd been away. She waved to Hal Barnett from Barnett's Drugs and Mindy Sloan, from the Book Nook. Cody's mother, Olive, arrived, along with Jennie Gray, who operated The Gables B and B.

Someone tapped her on the shoulder. Cody? No, Eva Townson gave her a hug and her husband, Mark, shook her hand. The couple owned the *Willow Beach Herald*, where Luci had interned.

"Haven't seen you since your homecoming party," Eva said. "How's the job going?"

"Ah, okay."

Eva raised an eyebrow. "Why am I not hearing *great* or *wonderful*?"

Luci shrugged. "Still getting used to it, I guess."

"I want to hear more," Eva said, "but now's not the time. We'll do lunch soon, okay?"

"Yes, I'd love that."

Eva moved away to speak to some newcomers. Luci watched her for a couple moments, thinking how much she owed Eva for mentoring her. She'd been so happy at the *Herald*. She was happy now, too.

Wasn't she?

Francine waved from across the room. She was with Ryan Talbot, her boss at the realty firm. Francine had her hair done up in a fancy twist. Her blue suit had a knee-length skirt and a jacket cinched in at the waist. Each time she saw Francine, she looked more beautiful and sophisticated.

Luci had dressed up, too. Instead of her usual slacks and blouse, she'd worn a suit. Although not as stylish as Francine's outfit, she thought it gave her a professional touch.

Her father and brother arrived. Erv looked neat and trim in dress pants, shirt and tie, and a light suit jacket. Don, who refused to comply with Erv's dress code, wore a short-sleeved sports shirt open at the neck with slacks.

Her father started "working the room," as he called it. Sometimes, when she saw him like this, he didn't seem like her father at all, but a stranger. She didn't know why that was. At home he was Dad, the man who played catch with his kids and made a mess in the kitchen when he cooked breakfast on Sundays. Here, he was Mr. Monroe, the Willow Beach National Bank president.

Glen called the meeting to order and, after the pledge to the flag, he invited everyone to visit the buffet table. Still no Cody. Luci tamped down her impatience. She loaded her plate with baked salmon, tossed salad and a roll and found an empty spot at one of the tables. Should she save Cody a place? No. Let him fend for himself. If he ever showed up.

After the meal, while people finished their desserts and refilled their coffee cups, Glen started the meeting. The agenda included the upcoming Fourth of July celebration, which featured a picnic in City Park followed by a fireworks display at the beach. Then they discussed the proposed roundabout at the intersection of Seabreeze Avenue and Main Street.

"And now we come to our August feature, the sand-castle contest," Glen said. "Our new PR Director, Luci Monroe, has an exciting innovation this year. You can read all about it in the next edition of our newsletter, which should be in your mailboxes—electronic or snail—in the next few days."

Luci barely had time to register that her ideas had been transformed from "is this the best you can do?" to "exciting," before the word *newsletter* rang in her brain.

The monthly newsletter. She'd been so preoccupied with the contest that she'd forgotten about that. Due in the next few days. Yikes.

"Some of you haven't met Luci yet," Glen was saying. "Stand up, Luci, and take a bow."

Luci stood and waved. "Thanks, Glen. Glad to be here."

"And, as many of you know, our photographer, Sam Reynolds, is taking the summer off. But not to worry, because filling in is the award-winning Cody Jarvis. He's also Olive's son. Cody, where are you? Give everyone a wave." Glen craned his neck and looked over the crowd. "Oh, there you are." He pointed to the back of the room.

Luci turned and saw Cody by the open door, leaning against the wall with his arms loosely folded. He dutifully waved.

How long had he been there?

When she turned back toward Glen, he handed the mike to her father.

"I want you all to help me celebrate today," Erv began, "because now all three of my children are members of the chamber of commerce. My son, Don, who works with me at the bank, my daughter Francine, who represents Talbot Realty, and now my daughter Luci, whom you just met. What a proud time this is for me, and for my wife, Anna."

Everyone clapped, and Luci had to stand again, along with Francine and Don.

When the meeting ended, her father motioned for the three of them to join him. "I want a picture of all of us," he said. He waved at Cody, who still stood near the door.

Cody raised his eyebrows. "Me?"

Erv nodded.

Cody glanced at the door and then at them. With a shrug, he ambled over.

"I want you to take our picture," Erv said. "You're the Chamber's official photographer, aren't you?"

"Ah, sure." Cody fussed with his camera.

Erv stood between Luci and Fran, his arms around their shoulders. Don stepped up next to Fran.

Standing in place, Cody snapped several shots. Which was odd, because usually he jumped around, arranging people in different poses and coaxing smiles.

After Cody had finished, Erv pulled him aside. Luci couldn't hear what they were talking about, but Cody looked grim. Then Glen walked by, and Erv turned away from Cody to ask, "Hey, Glen, how's my little girl doing?" He looped an arm around Luci's shoulder again.

"Dad!" Luci's face burned.

"Can't help it, I'm just so proud."

"She's a marvel." Glen slapped Erv on the back. "An absolute marvel."

Erv grinned and nodded. "That's what I wanted to hear."

"We still on for this Saturday?" Glen asked.

"Of course." Erv eased away from Luci to focus on Glen. "You want to try the new course at Hampton's Golf and Country? I have a client who belongs."

"Why, sure. I can make a hole in one there just as well as I can on our course."

Erv smirked. "Yeah, buddy. In your dreams."

While the two men continued their conversation, Luci exchanged a few words with

Francine and Don before they left. And then, turning to leave herself, she was suddenly face-to-face with Cody.

"Hey, Luci," he said. "You look great."

She brushed a piece of lint from her jacket sleeve and smoothed her skirt. "When you didn't show up on time, I decided you weren't coming."

"I told you I'd be here. I might not always *want* to do something, but if I say I will, I will."

"You missed lunch."

"I nibbled when I came in. I do have an excuse."

"Which you will undoubtedly download from your camera once you get home to your studio."

"No, I'm late because I had a flat tire."

She rolled her eyes. "Uh-huh."

"I did. Come on out to my rig and I'll show you." He gestured toward the door.

Luci stepped aside for a waiter holding a tray stacked with dishes. The room was rapidly emptying. She needed to get back to the office, too, and work on the newsletter. She began weaving her way through the tables toward the door.

Cody kept up with her.

"So where did this flat tire occur?" she asked.

"On the highway about five miles out of town."

She raised her eyebrows. "Mmm-hmm."

"Okay, so I did catch a couple tide pools this morning. But I had time to get back here for lunch. I just didn't plan on a flat tire. What? Did I miss anything important?"

She couldn't help laughing. "We're just so different. I thought being here was important."

"I know, and that's why I knocked myself out to make it. Didn't want to let you down."

"I appreciate that. I really do."

"I'm all yours," he said and then frowned, as though he'd let slip something he hadn't meant to say. But then his lips twitched with amusement. "For the rest of the day."

"Wouldn't want you to commit to anything more permanent than that," she said, matching his teasing tone and trying to keep a smile on her face.

CHAPTER EIGHT

"WHAT'S ON THE agenda this afternoon?" Cody asked. "Want to tackle the brochures? I could help with those."

Luci tossed her purse into a desk drawer and slammed it shut. "The newsletter is next. I forgot all about it, and it's due to be mailed in a few days. Shouldn't take long, though. The members have sent in their news, and I'll add a bit about the sand-castle contest. While I'm working on that, you could start on the brochures. That pile on the corner needs to be checked for updating."

She sat at her desk, turned on her computer and opened the file containing the members' news. When she looked up, Cody was fussing with his camera. She sighed.

"I want to show you something," he said, approaching her desk.

She wrinkled her brow. "Maybe we could look at your tide pools later?"

"Not the tide pools. Something else." He held the camera under her nose. "Recognize this?"

Without taking her hands from the keyboard, she studied the image on the screen. "Uh-huh. Calico Corner, the new store on Main Street. Where they sell handmade quilts and other crafts."

"Is the store mentioned in your newsletter?"

"Yes. The owner sent us an item about their grand opening. It's here somewhere." She scrolled through her file. "Here it is."

"You can use this photo."

"Hmm." Luci pressed a finger to her chin. "That would add interest."

"I have more of the businesses downtown, too." He showed her a dozen more shots of storefronts. "What do you think?"

"I think…yes, great idea for perking up the newsletter. But I don't remember us discussing this as a project."

"We didn't."

"So you were thinking of the newsletter, and this idea just popped into your head?"

He leaned against the corner of her desk. "I could lie and say yes to impress you, but that wasn't the case. When I was downtown one day, I spotted the Calico Corner and noticed how the light reflected on the quilt hanging in the front window. How vivid the colors were. And how the shadow from the roof made an interesting design on the brick wall. It all came together in a composition. So I captured it. And then I kept on walking, looking for other storefronts that spoke to me."

"That spoke to you?"

"Yeah. When you're writing, don't you sometimes hear the words clearly in your head, as though someone's saying them aloud?"

Luci sat back and folded her arms. "No, can't say that I have."

"Well, maybe someday you will. But what do you think? Want to use the pics or not?"

"Of course I do. They're wonderful. I just wish—" She bit her lower lip.

"What?"

"If I'd known what you were up to, I would've given you a list of the businesses—"

Cody shook his head. "Luci, I didn't plan to take those photos. It just happened."

"A good coincidence, then, that we were able to put the pictures to use."

He threw up his hands. "Have you ever heard of being spontaneous?"

"I don't call it spontaneity. I call it being disorganized."

"I give up," Cody said. "You'll never understand."

She sighed. "Probably not."

Later that afternoon, after Cody had left, Glen came by. He looked over her shoulder as she sat at the table proofreading the newsletter. "Ah, I see you've got that done. Good."

"Would you like to take a look?"

He waved a hand. "No, I'll wait. I've got a mountain of stuff to do."

Luci pictured Glen's shiny, bare desk and wondered where a "mountain" of work might be hiding. But perhaps he was a neat person who kept his work in desk drawers and files. Seeing Glen's gaze fastened on the mess on her worktable, she said, "I'm making headway, don't worry."

"You are? Doesn't look like it." He picked up a file folder and opened it, idly flipping through the contents. "Some of this could probably be tossed. But the minute we do that, someone will want it."

He replaced the file, cleared his throat and said, "Are you sure this job isn't too much for you, Luci?"

Luci tensed. "Why, no, not at all."

How could he say that, after all the praise he'd heaped on her at the chamber luncheon today? Was that only for her father's benefit?

"Never mind. Just asking. Want to be sure all my folks are happy here."

When he was gone, Luci sagged against the back of her chair. She didn't need more pressure, however subtle. And as far as being happy, she was. Even if Cody drove her crazy sometimes, and she was a little behind in her projects. Yes, she was happy.

Of course she was.

CODY GRABBED A duffel bag and stuffed it with a sweatshirt, a pair of jeans, socks and underwear. In his bathroom, he took a smaller bag already filled with toothbrush, toothpaste and other grooming necessities, and added it to the duffel. He pulled out his sleeping bag and case of extra lenses, film and a couple more cameras. While a pot of coffee brewed, he bagged up some crackers and apples and oranges. Cody was used to throwing things together for a spur-of-the-moment trip. He'd done it often enough.

His short visit to the tide pools, while refreshing, had only whetted his appetite for a longer getaway. He'd decided to take advantage of the upcoming weekend to do what he loved best: go on a picture hunt.

Twenty minutes later, he was traveling north along the highway. Once he'd left Willow Beach behind, he took a deep, relaxing breath and lightened his grip on the wheel. This was where he belonged.

His destination was a campground about three hours away, so he'd reach the front gate well before it was locked for the night. The grounds included a bluff overlooking the ocean and lots of wildlife. He might see some deer, even. There was a diner on the way where he could get takeout for his dinner. Later on, he'd haul his sleeping bag down to the beach, build a fire and watch the sun go down.

His thoughts turned to the chamber of commerce lunch. He really hadn't meant to be late, but neither was he particularly eager to attend. Not just because of the tide pools, but because Luci's father would be there. And, sure enough, he was. Cody had intended to avoid him, but he couldn't say no when Erv asked him to photograph him and his kids. Then, when Erv pulled him aside, Cody had braced himself for a remark about the scene in the diner, but Erv spoke only of the pictures Cody had just taken and how many copies he wanted.

Why was he so concerned, anyway? What Erv did was none of his business. Yet, he knew why: because of Luci. Because he cared about her, and because she had such a high regard for her family, especially for her father. He didn't want to see her disappointed.

There was still a chance he might be wrong...

His instincts told him he wasn't wrong.

Something was going on between the woman in the diner and Ervin Monroe.

THE TANGY SMELL of barbecue drifted through the house along with the sounds of talking and children's laughter. Luci smiled as she shut the door to her parents' house. This was how family Sundays should be, with everyone happy and having a good time. Last Sunday's disaster had been a fluke.

Luci continued down the hallway to the screened-in porch. The door was open and everyone was outside. That was to be expected, given today was barbecue day and her father was doing the honors. He loved to barbecue and had even created a recipe for his own sauce.

In one corner of the yard, Will tossed the Frisbee with his daughter, Betsy, and Don and Arliss's children, Spencer and Hannah. Betsy's younger sister, Megan, sat on the grass, watching. Arliss and Anna were arranging plates and silverware on the patio table, the paper tablecloth flapping in the stiff breeze. Don and Erv stood over the built-in barbecue pit, where smoke curled into the air. No Francine, but it was early yet. She'd be along.

As Luci approached Arliss and Anna, to see what she could do to help, she overheard her father say to Don, "You're not getting the loan, so quit asking."

Don folded his arms across his chest. "But I'm the loan officer."

"And I am the president of the bank, and I have the last word!"

"You give all your buddies a loan and not your own son?"

"Not for that broken-down piece of junk you call a boat. What are you thinking?"

"I'm thinking there are better things to do with my time than shuffle around your bank!" Don turned and stomped across the patio.

"Don, wait!" Luci called out. "What's going on?"

"Ask him." He pointed to Erv and then said to Arliss, "Come on, get the kids. We're outa here."

Arliss wrinkled her brow. "Don, simmer down, okay?"

He set his jaw. "So you side with them. Figures. Okay, I'm leaving." He turned and headed into the house.

Luci stared after him, unable to believe what was happening. In all the years of family Sundays, no one had ever walked out in anger. She turned to Arliss. "Why are they fighting?"

"Don wants to buy Ole Swenson's charter boat," Arliss said. She clutched her handful of silverware, her task forgotten. "But we need a loan to do it."

"Why does he want Ole's boat?"

Arliss shrugged. "He wants to run the charter business."

"I didn't send him to school to become a fisherman." Erv flipped a piece of chicken on the barbecue, and sparks shot into the air.

"What do you want him to do, Arliss?" Luci asked.

Arliss shrugged. "He does pretty much what he wants these days. But if he starts chartering, he'll be gone a lot."

Luci turned to Will, who had stepped onto the patio to pull a can of soda from the cooler. "You work at the marina. What do you think of Ole's boat?"

Will snapped the soda open and took a sip. "Haven't had a look at its engine. Couldn't say."

Luci and Arliss helped Anna bring out the salad and rolls and a tray of fresh vegetables and dip, and Will took Don's place as Erv's helper with the barbecue. Maybe they could salvage the day, after all.

But, when the chicken was done, Erv pulled a chair up to the end of the patio and sat by himself. Anna chose a seat at the table. Will took his plate inside and sat in front of the TV. Arliss beckoned the children to a blanket she'd spread on the grass.

Seeing Megan lag behind, Luci grabbed her hand. "Let's eat together, okay?" She pointed to a wrought-iron table and two chairs.

"Okay." Megan looked glum, but she trotted obediently along with Luci.

Luci fixed their plates and, when they were settled at the table, she asked, "Are you having fun this summer?"

Megan poked her fork at a piece of chicken. "Sometimes. 'Cept when the others won't let me play. They say I'm too little."

"I'm sorry," Luci said. "Tell you what. When we're done eating, let's you and I play checkers. I hear you're hard to beat."

That brought a smile to Megan's lips.

But when dinner was over, before Luci could take out the checkerboard, Will said, "Time for me and the girls to split. Got stuff to do at home."

They'd barely left when Don phoned Arliss on her cell and said he was out front to pick up her and the kids. "I need to help clean up," she told him.

Anna shook her head and said, "I can handle it. You go on home."

After Arliss and the children left, Erv scrubbed the barbecue and then disappeared into his study. Anna told Luci she didn't have to help in the kitchen, but Luci insisted.

They worked in silence while Luci loaded the dishwasher and Anna put away the leftovers. Presently, Anna said, "Don't worry about your brother and dad. They'll work it out."

"I don't know… I've never seen Don so angry. I thought he liked being a banker."

Anna spooned the leftover salad into a smaller bowl and clamped on the plastic lid. "The trouble between Don and your dad has been brewing for a long time. You've been away and haven't been aware that Don wanted to change his profession. You can't blame Dad for being disappointed. He put a lot of effort into getting all you kids established."

"I know, and I'm glad Francine's doing well, but she's married to her job. She never even showed up today. How long is Will going to put up with her being gone so much?" Luci took the empty salad bowl and added it to the dishwasher.

"I'm sure he's proud of her and her success."

"Maybe so, but—"

"Just like I'm proud of you. And so is your dad. He's so pleased that you're with the chamber."

"Me, too. But, Mom, our family—"

"Will be fine, honey. Just fine." She was smiling, but as she turned away, her smile faded.

LATER, AS LUCI stepped inside her apartment, she breathed a sigh of relief. Once again, family Sunday had been a time of discord rather than harmony. Her family had always provided a refuge, a place where she felt safe and protected. Where she belonged. Tonight, she couldn't wait to escape.

Maybe a walk on the beach would help. She grabbed a hooded sweater and went outside.

Luci stood on her patio a moment, watching the dune grasses sway in the breeze like dancers in perfect unison. The sun sat on the horizon amid a few puffy clouds. A gull cawed, sounding forlorn. Luci sighed. She knew she shouldn't feel sorry for herself, but she couldn't help it.

She started along the path through the dunes, head down, hands buried in her sweater pockets. Maybe she shouldn't have come back to Willow Beach. Maybe she didn't belong here, after all. She'd so looked forward to being here, to taking her place in the family, in the community. But her job wasn't what she'd thought it would be, and now it appeared the family wasn't, either.

But if she didn't belong here, where did she belong?

She reached the sand and plowed through the soft part to the hard-packed shore, where walking was easier. Luci passed a few other people she didn't know, but she exchanged smiles and hellos anyway. In the distance, the lighthouse's rotating beacon brightened the darkening sky.

Gradually, her taut nerves began to unwind and she felt better. Not great, but better. She turned around and started back to her apartment. Stars popped out as the sky faded from blue to black. Her front door came into view.

Not quite ready to go in, she stopped at the

path leading to her patio and sat in the still-warm sand with her back against a log. The peaceful evening began to work its magic, as she knew it would. The only thing missing was someone to share these moments. She'd dated a few men while at the U, but no one who lasted. And Ben Shapiro wasn't the one, not that she wanted him to be.

Cody's image popped into her mind. No, he wasn't her type, either. Yet, she'd had a crush on him. That just proved how irrational crushes were. They were part of growing up, something you got over when you were older.

"Hey, Luci."

Cody? She peered into the semidarkness. Sure enough, there he was, loping along the path to her apartment. What was he doing here?

She made a move to rise, but he put out a hand.

"Don't get up. I'll join you—if that's okay."

"All right. Have a seat." She settled back against the log and patted the sand beside her. "Did you come on a mission?"

Cody sat and folded his long legs, clasping his arms around his knees. "No, just passing by on my way home, saw your car and decided to say hello. When you didn't answer the bell, I figured you were out here on the beach."

"On your way home?"

"Yeah. I took another trip, a longer one. I headed off on Friday, after I left the chamber office. I needed to get out of town for a while."

"Where'd you go?"

"Up the coast to the campground."

"Get some good pictures? Silly question, huh?"

He grinned. "Yeah, but I don't mind you asking. I'll show them to you later."

"When you're out on an assignment, where do you usually stay?"

"Wherever I can. When we were in Canada to catch the snow geese, we stayed in a motel. If the weather is good enough, we might camp out. Like I did last night."

She wondered if "we" meant women, too, but didn't want to ask. She couldn't imagine life as a constant campout.

They watched a pair of gulls circle and fly away, and then he said, "So, how's the family? Did you have your usual Sunday dinner?"

"We did." She sobered at the memory.

"You don't sound happy about it. Is everyone okay?"

"If you mean is anyone sick, the answer is no."

"Then what?"

She twisted her fingers together, debating whether or not to confide in him. Finally, she said, "Oh, there were the usual arguments among the kids. The older ones pick on Megan. I guess kids arguing is to be expected, though."

"Not having any brothers or sisters, I don't know. Did you and Don and Francine argue when you were growing up?"

"Yes, we fought, sometimes. But on the whole, we got along."

"One big happy family."

When she remained silent, he said, "You are, aren't you?"

"Sure, we are." Her voice sounded hollow, even to her own ears.

He studied her. "Luci, are you okay?"

"Yes... No."

"Want to tell me about it?"

"I don't know. I've always been taught not to tell family business. But you're..." She almost said *practically family* but stopped herself in time and instead finished with "Don's friend."

"Yep. We've been friends for a long time. Does what you're concerned about have to do with him?"

"Partly. Don and Dad had a horrible argument today. Don wants a bank loan to buy Ole Swensen's charter boat, and Dad refuses. Did you know about Don and this boat?"

"Yeah, he mentioned it one day."

"I can't believe he'd seriously consider quitting his job at the bank to operate a charter fishing boat. What do you think?"

Cody unclasped his knees and leaned back against the log. "I'm a bad one to ask, Luci, because I believe you're supposed to find what you love to do in life and then do it."

"Even if it affects other people? Like a wife and children? Your parents?"

"That's the part I haven't figured out yet. Probably because I don't have a wife and children. I have Mom, of course. And, yeah, she's sad when I leave, and she nags me about getting married."

"She does?"

"Uh-huh, even though she knows it won't do any good."

"You'll never marry? How can you say that? Maybe someone will come along and you'll fall madly in love. Maybe you'll even make sacrifices for her and the children."

Cody threw back his head and laughed. "At this point, I hardly know what I'm doing tomorrow. And, besides, we were talking about your family, not my nonexistent one."

"I know. I'm not sure why I'm telling you all this, anyway."

"Because we're friends, and we've known each other for a long time. And I'm hoping Don and Arliss will work out all their problems."

"I suppose every relationship, every marriage hits some bumps now and then."

He was silent a moment and then cast her a sideways glance. "But Erv and Anna, they're still tight, aren't they?"

Something in his voice put her on alert. She tried to meet his gaze, but he was looking down, poking a stick into the sand. "Yes," she said, "they're fine. They've always been great role models for us. But why do you ask?"

He gave a dismissive wave. "Just throwing that into the pot. For discussion's sake."

Afterward, when Cody had gone and she was putting on her pajamas, Luci thought about his question regarding her parents. She was thankful they were okay. If something were to threaten their solid relationship, there'd probably be no hope for any of them.

CODY PULLED HIS duffel and sleeping bags from the SUV and carried them into his apartment. Hard to believe his getaway was over already. But here he was back in Willow Beach. However short, the trip had been a good one, and he'd taken some awesome pictures.

As he unpacked, his thoughts settled on his visit to Luci. His stopping by hadn't been quite as impromptu as he'd wanted her to believe. Something had happened on his way home that reinforced his concerns about Erv Monroe.

When he'd reached Oceanside, he'd stopped to grab a coffee and stretch his legs. He'd walked by the amusement park, which had a mini–Ferris wheel and a train that ran around the perimeter. Music blasted from elevated loudspeakers, and the aromas of cotton candy and popcorn floated along the airwaves.

Cody had strolled along, sipping his coffee, getting a kick out of the kids as they ran here and there to take the various rides. At one point, he'd stopped to watch the Dodge 'Em track, where miniature cars, airplanes and trucks zigzagged around.

After a while, ready to move on, he turned away—and looked directly into the eyes of the woman standing next to him. Her short stature and gray hair struck a chord—but it was her cane that confirmed her identity.

She was Erv's "client."

Her eyes lit with recognition. "Hello," she said pleasantly. "Aren't you Cody? Erv's friend. You work with his daughter, Luci."

"I am. And you obviously know more about me than I do about you."

"I'm Helen Stevens."

When she volunteered nothing more, he said, "Erv's client."

She laughed. "Is that what he told you?"

"Well, it's really none of my—"

"We're old friends, Erv and I."

"I see. You live here in Oceanside?"

"I'm just visiting... Oh, the ride's over. I need to watch for Jason." She turned toward the Dodge 'Em track.

"Sure. Nice meeting you, Helen."

She put out a hand to stop him. "Don't leave yet. I want you to meet him."

As the kids streamed from the ride, a boy of about six or seven broke away and ran up. "Grandma, Grandma, here I am."

She caught him with her free hand and pulled him close. "Jason, I want you to meet someone. This is Cody."

The boy looked up at Cody and held out his hand. "Pleased t' meet you, Cody."

Cody shook his hand. "Good to meet you, too, Jason." There was something familiar about him, but Cody couldn't pin it down.

"I didn't ride in a car. I rode an airplane."

"Jason loves airplanes." Helen smoothed his cowlick.

"I'm going to be a pilot someday," Jason said and tugged on Helen's hand. "Can I go on another ride, Grandma?"

"One more," she said, "and then we have to go. Mavis is waiting for us." She turned to Cody. "Nice to meet you, Cody."

"You, too, Helen."

Helen and her grandson had preoccupied Cody the rest of the way home. She'd said she was an old friend of Erv's. But how old? And how good a friend? By the time he reached Willow Beach, he'd decided to drive by Luci's and if possible talk to her. He couldn't shake the feeling trouble was brewing.

CHAPTER NINE

"GOOD MORNING, LUCI." Glen's voice boomed through the doorway to Luci's office.

Luci rose from her seat and turned to greet her boss. Then she saw that he wasn't alone. A girl of about sixteen or seventeen followed him into the room, frowning and crossing her arms over her chest.

"I'm doing just fine, Mr... Glen. The newsletter went out, the sand-castle contest is shaping up, and I'm planning the article for next month's *Coastal Living*."

"Hmm, I want to talk to you about that. But not now. Meet Tessa." He stood aside, allowing the girl and Luci to face each other. "Tessa, this is Luci Monroe. She's your boss. I want you to do what she says, and I want to hear from her that you're doing a good job."

"Hi, Luci," Tessa said in a monotone.

Glen's announcement left Luci speechless. She quickly recovered, though, and said,

"Pleased to meet you, Tessa." She turned to Glen. "Have we discussed this?"

He rubbed his chin. "Hmm, it may have slipped my mind. The last few days have been hectic. But you can use some help, is that right?"

"I suppose she could do some filing and answer the phone when I'm gone."

"How you use her skills is up to you."

"Do I have to stay here all day, Uncle Glen?" Tessa asked. "If I do, I'll never have any fun this summer."

Uncle Glen. Okay, now this was beginning to make sense.

"You'll have the weekends for fun." He tapped his wristwatch. "I need to leave now."

And, before Luci or Tessa could say any more, he was gone.

"So, what do you want me to do?" Tessa fiddled with the skinny braid dangling at the side of her face. The rest of her cocoa-brown hair was shoulder length. At least some of it was. With her choppy haircut, it was difficult to tell.

"Give me a minute here," Luci said. "This is so unexpected."

Tessa snorted. "You're telling me. I just

got here Friday and I already have a job? I wasn't planning on working, period. This is summer, for goodness' sake."

"Let's sit down for a few minutes and get acquainted." Luci gestured to the table.

Arms hugging her waist, flip-flops slapping on the tile floor, Tessa crossed the room and slumped into a chair. She smoothed her orange T-shirt over her jeans and settled her small cloth shoulder purse on her lap.

Luci pulled out a chair and sat beside her. "So you're visiting your uncle?"

"No, I got dumped on my father this summer. He's Uncle Glen's younger brother. Way younger. My mom and dad are divorced, and my mom's on a trip with her boyfriend. She told my dad he had to take me for the rest of the summer. And he works all day at the marina."

"Where are you from?"

"Portland. I've been here before, though. I know some kids in town." She gestured at the piles on the table. "Is that the junk I'm supposed to clean up? Uncle Glen said your office was a mess."

"He said that?"

"Uh-huh, and that this was a good place

to keep me out of trouble. I don't know why he said that, unless he meant Carl."

"Carl?"

"A guy I know. He thinks he's my boyfriend. Oh, there he is now." She pointed to the window.

Sure enough, a young man stood outside in the courtyard. He appeared to be a few years old than Tessa. His sleeveless T-shirt reached past his knees, nearly covering his cargo pants, and his hair stood up in gelled spikes. He waved with one hand, fingers spread.

"He shouldn't bother you at work," Luci said.

"Oh, he won't bother me."

"I don't think your uncle Glen would approve of Carl hanging around. And I don't, either."

"Oops, you're right. And Uncle Glen would tell my dad, and I'd be in deep trouble." She unzipped her purse and pulled out her phone. "I'll text Carl that I'll meet him for lunch. What time is lunch?"

"Twelve o'clock. But if I'm gone during that time, you'll need to be here."

"Not today, though?" She looked up with a hopeful expression.

"No, not today, this being your first day."

"All right!" She smiled and then tapped out her text.

Carl pulled his phone from a side pocket in his cargo pants, read the screen and, without looking up, tapped out a reply. Then he gave a salute and ambled off toward the courtyard's exit.

Luci breathed a sigh of relief. "Be sure to tell Carl that hanging around while you're working isn't appropriate."

"I'll tell him," Tessa promised. "But he's got a mind of his own."

"We might as well get you started. A good place to begin is the filing cabinets over there." Luci pointed to the row of cabinets lining one wall. "They need cleaning out."

"Ick."

"Then we can start putting away this *information*." She stressed the word, hoping Tessa took the hint that the material was not to be referred to as "junk."

"Have you had any experience filing?"

"No, but I know my ABC's, so it can't be too hard."

"I want you to take out material from the file drawers and sort it on the table, putting related things together. Like past issues of *Coastal Life*." She went to the files, pulled an issue from one of the drawers and held it up. "Then I'll take a look and decide what to keep and what to discard."

"So I'm a file clerk. I thought I was your assistant. That's what Uncle Glen said."

"He also said I get to decide how to use your skills. Shall we get started?"

LUCI RETURNED TO her work but found it difficult to concentrate with Tessa banging drawers and shuffling back and forth across the room in her flip-flops. When Glen stuck his head in the door and said, "Luci, I need to see you in my office," she welcomed the chance to take a break.

Once settled with his shiny desk between them, she expected him to talk about Tessa, perhaps give her pointers on how to manage the difficult teen. But no, he launched into something else.

"You said you'd chosen the topic for the next article in *Coastal Living*."

"Yes, the lighthouse. They've made the

keeper's house into a rental and added a souvenir store. Lots of news there."

"I want you to put that aside for the next issue and write about the resort at Pine Lake."

"All right… Is there something special you want me to focus on?"

"Yes, what a popular place it is."

"But is it still? I thought it was rather run-down."

"Still popular. Make it look good. Get Cody cracking with the photos. He can do wonders."

Luci returned to her office to find Tessa sitting at the table bent over her phone. When she saw Luci, Tessa blushed and tucked her phone away.

"What did Uncle Glen say about me?"

"Not a word," Luci said.

"Oh, good. I see it's time for lunch. One hour, right? I'll be back at one."

"Without Carl," Lucy cautioned.

"Yeah. But, like I say, he's got a mind of his own."

Luci went to the café next door for a tuna sandwich and a cup of coffee. She took the food back to her office and, while she ate, spent considerable time canceling the interviews she'd scheduled at the lighthouse and making a new appointment with Mike Baxter, Pine Lake Resort's owner.

LUCI LOOKED AT her watch for the fourth time in the past ten minutes. *Come on, Cody, show up.* The drive to Pine Lake would take at least half an hour. Knowing Cody, though, she should have allowed more time.

"What, you got a hot date?" Tessa, her arms full of folders, was grinning at her.

"No, why do you say that?"

"'Cause you keep looking at your watch."

"I have an appointment for an interview, and I'm waiting for— Oh, here he is now."

Cody stepped into the office. "Hey, Luci."

"Finally."

"What? Am I late?"

"No, no, you're fine. Come and meet Tessa. Tessa, this is Cody."

The two greeted each other, with Tessa offering the kind of grin Luci had only seen her display when Carl was mentioned.

"Are you Luci's assistant, too?" Tessa dumped her armload of files on the table, where they scattered in all directions.

Cody tossed his head back and laughed. "You'll have to ask Luci about that."

"I'm supposed to be her assistant, but I'm really the file drudge." She wrinkled her nose.

Cody laughed some more, while Luci straightened the files Tessa had spilled and then picked up her purse and tablet. "If anyone calls, take a message, please," Luci told Tessa.

"Okay, but if you aren't back by quitting time, I'm still outa here."

"That's fine. Marge will lock up. She stays till six."

"So where should I say you are? To the people who phone." Tessa twisted her braid around her finger.

"You don't. You just say I'm out and take a message."

Once they had left the building and were on their way to Cody's SUV, he said, "Wow, when did that happen?"

"Tessa? Glen brought her in yesterday." She filled him in on Tessa's background.

"She's got an attitude," he said.

"That she didn't waste any time showing."

"She could be helpful, though."

They rounded the building and entered the parking lot. Luci spotted Cody's black SUV a couple rows over.

"I didn't know I needed help. Except yours. Which is challenge enough."

"Come on, I can already tell I'm a piece of cake compared to her."

"She comes with a boyfriend, too." She told him about Carl.

"Tall, skinny dude with spiky hair?"

"Yes, that sounds like him."

Cody nodded. "I saw him hanging around the entrance when I came in."

"I hope he doesn't actually go in the office while I'm gone."

"Doubt he'd get past Marge."

"You're right—she's a guard dog."

He opened the passenger door of his SUV, and she slipped onto the seat. His rolled-up sleeping bag was still in the back, atop the locked box that stored his equipment.

"You should get yourself a trailer or a small motor home," she said when he'd climbed into the driver's seat.

He shook his head. "Even this rig is more than I want to carry around. But I've got to have someplace for all my gear." He started the engine. "So what's with the switch from the lighthouse to Pine Lake?"

"Glen's request. Or, rather, his orders. I wasn't given a choice."

"I thought Pine Lake was about ready to close down. Last time I was there, hardly any of the cabins were rented."

Luci placed her purse on the floor and settled back in her seat. "I haven't been there for a long time, but I've heard they aren't doing well. Still, Glen insists we do a feature on them."

"Well, the chamber exists to promote local businesses," Cody said.

"I know, but I think something else is going on here."

"You think he has an ulterior motive?" Cody pulled out of the parking lot and onto Main Street.

"I am suspicious."

They rode along in silence for a few miles, and then Cody said, "Got all your questions written?"

She tapped her tablet. "You bet I do. And I'm sure you have all your photos planned."

"Oh, yeah."

He met her gaze for a second or two, and

they both laughed. Then he said, "Seriously, I suppose you want to keep me on a short leash."

"Hmm, does that mean you can be trained, after all?"

"Well...probably not."

"I figured."

Although they'd kept the conversation light, Luci sensed their words carried a serious undertone. Maybe they'd better quit while they were ahead. She folded her arms and turned toward the window, hoping to discourage further conversation. He apparently took the hint and fell silent, too.

They reached the turnoff to Pine Lake and a few minutes after that came upon the lake and the resort. Accommodations consisted of a dozen or so log cabins that were best described as "rustic," and a parking lot for motor homes and trailers. Only two motor homes occupied the lot. A small café and a boat rental and bait shop were nearby. A few people were around, some carrying fishing poles and a couple with picnic baskets, but not as many as Luci would expect during the peak of the summer season.

Cody parked in the motor home lot and

they got out of the SUV. The air was drier than in Willow Beach, and the scent of pine replaced that of salt water.

"Who're we looking for?" Cody asked as he looped the camera strap around his neck.

"Mike Baxter, the resort owner. And I think that's him." She pointed to a man standing at the edge of the lake. Arms folded and feet spread apart, he was gazing at the water as though lost in thought.

"Mr. Baxter?" she asked when they'd reached the man's side.

He turned and frowned. "Yeah, I'm Mike Baxter."

"We're from the Willow Beach Chamber of Commerce," Luci said. "I called you yesterday about an interview for *Coastal Living.*"

"Oh, right."

"Is this a bad time?" Luci asked when Mike continued to frown while they all exchanged handshakes. "I know I just called you yesterday, but our deadline—"

"No, no, this is fine. I'm just preoccupied, trying to figure out how to keep this place going." He ran a hand over his gray crew cut and heaved a sigh. "We used to turn people away this time of year. Now we've got a seventy-five percent vacancy."

"Why's that?" Cody asked.

Mike shrugged. "Lots of reasons, I suppose. There's a new place on the other side of the lake with fancier accommodations and more boats. We need to remodel here but can't afford to right now. Anyway, Glen said the article in *Coastal Living* should help. Long as you keep it upbeat. So don't quote anything I just said."

"We'll do the best we can," Luci said.

She took out her tape recorder and switched it on. Then she and Mike Baxter strolled the shore while she conducted her interview. Or tried to. He kept interrupting to ask how answering a particular question would help him get more business. Cody disappeared, as expected, but he returned to take Mike's photo. When he posed, Mike's smile and proud stance gave no indication of his troubles.

Mike excused himself to attend to something in the office, and Luci and Cody walked around together. In the picnic area, where tall pine trees shaded tables and barbecue pits, they found a family who agreed to be interviewed and photographed. They were enthusiastic about the resort and gave Luci some good quotes for her article.

When they were ready to leave, they found Mike in the office, peering at his computer screen through black-framed glasses. He punched a couple of keys and then gave them his attention. "Another cancellation."

"Sorry to hear that," Luci said. "But we're leaving now, and we wanted to thank you for the interview."

"I hope the article works."

"Glen must be a good friend of yours to be helping you out like this."

"Friend?" Mike snorted. "I don't know about that. But he *should* want to help. He's half owner of this place."

Luci gritted her teeth as she followed Cody to his SUV and climbed in. As he slid behind the wheel, he glanced at her but didn't say anything. She folded her arms and stared out the window.

Neither spoke until they hit the highway, and then Cody said, "You're bummed out, aren't you?"

"Yes, I am. I resent Glen using me—and you, too—for his own ends."

Cody swung into the inside lane to pass a slow-moving truck. "So, what are you going to do?"

"I could quit, I suppose, but I don't want to. I've been looking forward to coming home and working for the chamber. You probably don't understand because you move around from job to job."

"That doesn't mean I don't run into difficult people and frustrations. But that's life. People aren't perfect, Luci, even if you'd like them to be."

"So, I'm supposed to lower my standards. Is that what you're saying?"

Cody let a few seconds elapse, and then he said, "Here's what I would do. Forget about Glen and Baxter and their agenda, and concentrate on writing the best article you can. I'll send you my photos, and when you're ready, we can sit down together. Like we did with the article on Cranberry Acres."

Luci allowed a smile to reach her lips. "Well, how can I turn down an offer like that?"

He must have picked up on her teasing tone, because he laughed and said, "Yup, and

I don't make an offer like that to just any-one."

She rolled her eyes. "Wow, I feel so spe-cial."

"You are, Luci," he said softly. "You are."

CHAPTER TEN

Luci sat at her desk, working on the Pine Lake article. Or trying to. Mostly, she'd been staring at the screen. She wanted to follow Cody's suggestion and forget about Glen and Mike Baxter and concentrate on the writing. Easier said than done.

"What's the matter?"

Tessa's voice brought Luci to her senses. She looked around to see Tessa standing behind her. "Working on my article about Pine Lake," she said, minimizing the file on her screen.

"Writer's block?" Tessa smiled as though that was something good.

"No!" Luci's protest came out sharper than she'd intended.

"Use lots of quotes," Tessa said. "Short sentences and lots of white space. That's what my English teacher told us. People today have short attention spans, she said."

"I'll keep that in mind," Luci said. "How are you doing with the files?"

"The files are a mess." Tessa threw up her hands and sighed.

"Well, now, that's why we have you, isn't it?" Her resistance down, Luci had let a note of sarcasm creep into her voice. Then she pasted a smile on her face. "I really need to get back to work here."

"Okay. It's time for my break, anyway. All right if I go get a soda?"

"Yes, go. And say hi to Carl for me." At Tessa's raised eyebrows, Luci added, "I saw him lounging in the lobby when I came back from lunch."

"I told him not to look in the window at us anymore."

"Thanks. I appreciate that."

As Tessa's footsteps faded down the hallway, Luci sat back and exhaled. She rested a moment and then read over what she'd written. Her words made little sense. She hadn't been able to concentrate with Tessa slamming file drawers and shuffling back and forth across the room. That was her excuse, anyway.

What to do now? She eyed the file cabinets.

Maybe she should take a turn at straightening the files. Putting things in order gave her a sense of control. But, no, she didn't want to risk Tessa coming back and discovering her at that task. She put her fingers on the keyboard again. *Concentrate, Luci, concentrate.*

"My DREAM JOB is turning into a nightmare," Luci said. She sighed and picked at her crab salad, her appetite gone.

"I'm sorry to hear that," Eva said.

Charlie's Fish House was packed, as usual. Talk, laughter and the clink of cutlery on dishes surrounded them, blending with the hum of the ocean.

Luci had planned to relax and enjoy her time with Eva, but as soon as she sat down she'd started spilling her problems. "I'm sorry to be such a complainer," she said.

Eva finished a bite of her shrimp. "Don't apologize. I want to know how your job is going. I like to think I played a role in your career choice."

"Oh, you did. A big role. I don't know what I would have done without you—and your father. He was my first mentor, and when he passed away, you came along to take his place."

"Having you as an intern was great. We had fun doing the fashion shows for the high school."

"And the article I wrote about it for the *Herald* was my first published piece of journalism. That wouldn't have happened without you, Eva."

"I was glad to be there for you."

"You seem to have found your dream job." Luci broke a roll and spread butter on one half. "It all worked out perfectly for you."

Eva sipped her iced tea and set the glass on the table. "Now, wait a minute, my dear. Life is not a static thing where you reach a goal and then that's it. Life is a continual process of adjustment and problem solving."

"You mean your life isn't perfect?" Luci was teasing again.

"Not by a long shot. Sasha's going to be a teenager soon. Do you know what that means? Boys—and dating. Yikes."

Luci grinned. "Oh, you poor thing. But she's always been a good daughter. And I bet Elijah is growing to be a good son. He's how old now?"

"Going on four and quite the little man already. But let's get back to you. You say Tessa is Glen's niece?"

"Yes, and I can understand her not wanting to be here." She explained Tessa's family situation. "But we have a job to do. I thought maybe I could mentor her, like you did me, but I lose patience."

"It might help if you could find something she's especially good at, or give her jobs with more responsibility, where she can be successful. Keep trying. But remember, too, that you're the boss."

They stopped talking while the waiter refilled their glasses with iced tea. When he left, Eva said, "How are you and Cody getting along? If you want to talk about it."

Luci's stomach tensed. "That's another problem."

"I'd be glad to listen. But I suppose you have a lot of people to serve as a sounding board. Your family is so close…"

Luci looked away, idly watching two girls scamper hand in hand across the sand. She and Francine used to play like that when they were little, she thought with a rush of sadness. And now they barely had time for each other.

She turned back to Eva. "Some problems are hard to talk about, even to the people who are closest to us."

"That's true enough. So, I'm listening."

"Thanks, Eva." Luci took a deep breath and said, "He's always made it clear that we're only friends. But there's a part of me that doesn't want to give up hoping. I wish I could turn off my feelings, but I don't seem to be able to."

"Those kinds of feelings are the hardest to control. They're either there or they aren't."

"And when Glen hired him as photographer and made it clear we were supposed to be a team, I was back to square one, so to speak."

"Thank you, Glen Thomas."

"So here I am struggling just like I did in high school and college. Trouble is, I can't tell if my feelings are still a crush or if I'm actually in love with him."

Eva sat back. "Wow, you do have a dilemma."

"Plus, our styles are so different. I like to have a plan and he's spur-of-the-moment.

How did you ever put up with him when he worked for you?"

"We pretty much let him do his own thing. But all the traveling and job-hopping he's done since then may have made him even more independent. But you and Cody aren't the only ones whose work styles clash. When Mark and I first met, we were at odds over how to run the newspaper."

"And now you're perfect together. How did you get to be such a good team?"

Eva's eyes twinkled. "Our relationship outside the office may have had something to do with it."

"No chance of that with me and Cody. He'll be leaving at the end of the summer, and I'll be staying here in Willow Beach. This is where I've always wanted to be."

The waiter brought their checks. "This has been nice," Eva said as she pulled her wallet from her purse. "I'm glad we could get together."

Luci paid her bill and left a tip for the waiter. "So am I. But I feel like I dumped all my problems on you."

"And I didn't solve any of them." Eva stood and pushed in her chair.

"You listened, though. I appreciate that."
Luci joined Eva as they crossed the deck to
the stairs leading to the street.

"I'm always here to listen," Eva said.

When they reached the sidewalk, they
hugged and promised to lunch again soon.
Eva turned toward the *Herald*'s office, while
Luci went in the opposite direction toward
the chamber.

What a good friend Eva had become. In
ways, Luci felt closer to her than her own
family. More and more, her family was turning into strangers.

CHAPTER ELEVEN

"So what do you think of my place?" Cody stood aside while Luci walked around his apartment. He hoped he hadn't missed anything when he'd cleaned up for her visit. Photography magazines neatly stacked on the table? Check. Kitchen sink free of dirty dishes? Check. Groceries stowed away? Check.

Uh-oh, there was a towel on the floor. He snatched it up and slapped it on the towel rack. Then he propped his hands on his hips and focused on her again. She'd changed from her work outfit into jeans and a T-shirt and left her hair loose instead of pulling it back into its usual ponytail. He liked her casual look.

Finally, she said, "It's so…so *you*."

He frowned. "What exactly does that mean?"

She looked at him with earnest eyes. "I meant it as a compliment. It's the kind of place I would expect you to have. You're surrounded by everything that's important to you." She waved at the shelves displaying his cameras, lenses, tripods and other equipment.

"How do you like my photos?" he said. "That one I took in the Alps. And that's from my gig in Alaska. Check out the antlers on that moose." He went around the room, giving her a tour.

When he'd finished, she said, "We'd better get to work."

"Oh, yeah. Sorry, I tend to get carried away."

He hadn't invited her over to brag about his work. He'd thought it would be easier to collaborate with his computer set up. Cody had several screens that were bigger than those at the office or at her place.

If he had any other motive for having her here, he refused to think about what that might be.

"We'll put your article on that screen," he said, "and my photos over there and see what we've got."

That accomplished, he scrolled through her article and then sat silent.

"You don't like it," she said.

"No, I'm thinking. Go back to the part where you talk about families having fun."

She found the place. "I was trying to honor Mike's request that we emphasize the family angle."

"And you did. And so did I." He flipped through his photos until he came to the one he wanted. "What do you think of this?"

She leaned forward to look. "The couple with the little boy. I remember them. Okay, he's digging in the sand and the mom's spreading a blanket and the dad is setting down the picnic basket."

"Notice the background?"

"The rowboats."

"I was showing as much going on as I could without faking it," Cody said.

"I think you succeeded."

They continued on, mixing and matching text with photos. Presently, there was a knock on the door.

Luci looked up. "Are you expecting anyone?"

"No, I'm not." Cody went to the door and opened it to find his mother standing there. She held a napkin-covered tray.

"Thought you two might like a little snack."

Without waiting to be invited in, Olive stepped past Cody and headed for the kitchen area, pausing to nod at Luci. "So good to see you. And welcome to the chamber, by the way."

"Thanks, Olive."

"I hope this one isn't giving you a bad time," she said.

Luci laughed. "Not so far."

"When you get hungry, dig in to these sandwiches and veggies. And chocolate cake for dessert—baked today."

Olive fussed with the food, arranging and rearranging the dishes. Finally, she said, "I'll be going now. Let me know if you want seconds on anything."

"Will do, Mom."

He had to smile as he saw his mother to the door. When he'd told her Luci was coming over, she'd clapped her hands and said, "Oh, joy."

"Not what you think," he'd told her. "It's a work session."

"I'm glad you work well together."

"We don't. That's the point. I'm trying to get the job done with as little pain as possible."

But she'd just smiled.

After his mother left, he turned to Luci. "What can I say? She's a mom."

"She's sweet," Luci said.

They worked for another half hour and then stopped to eat.

When they were finished, she carried their plates to the sink.

"Just leave them," he said, "and we can get back to work."

"Actually, I'd better go." She kept her back to him as she stood at the sink.

"What? We're not done." He went to stand beside her, and she stepped away.

"I should go," she repeated, her head down as she rinsed the plates.

"Why? Do you have a date?"

"No," she said, annoyance coloring her voice. "Do you?"

"This is the best date I've had in ages!" He expected her to laugh at his joke, feeble though it was, but her face took on a stricken look. Oh, man, had he hurt her feelings? He hadn't meant to. He was about to tell her he was only teasing, but before he could, she'd shut off the water and hurried to the worktable.

"I'll download what we've done so far and take it from here."

He wanted to protest, but her decisive tone told him to back off.

After she left, he stood there staring at the door and listening to the sound of her car starting up and pulling out of the driveway.

LUCI PARKED, CUT the engine and sat there, barely noticing the spectacular sunset. What was wrong with her? Why had she let Cody's remark set her off?

Was it because deep down she wished they *had* been on a date?

Whatever the reason, she'd had to get out of his apartment. Being there with him was too personal, too cozy. They needed to work together at the office, where she could keep her distance—physically and emotionally.

Inside her apartment, she switched on a table lamp, and her gaze fell on the yellow bowl her mother had given her. She sat on the sofa and picked up the bowl, running her fingers over the smooth surface. She put it down and paged through the album Cody had made her. Everyone looked so happy celebrating her return to Willow Beach. Who would have guessed that barely a month later, her family—and her dream—would be falling apart.

CODY DROVE THROUGH town looking for a place to park. He'd been working at home sorting through pictures and had become restless. So he'd put on a jacket, grabbed a camera and jumped in the car. He thought about driving out of town but nixed that idea. He needed to be at work tomorrow at the chamber. Willow Beach would have to do for tonight.

Driving along Main Street, he spotted an empty space at the curb and pulled into it. He cut the engine and sat there staring out the windshield. What was he doing? What did he want to do? Just get out of the car, an inner voice commanded. So he did. He locked the car and stood on the sidewalk wondering where to go. Have a cup of coffee? No, he'd had enough coffee at home. Have a beer? Sitting on a barstool didn't hold much appeal, either.

Okay, just walk.

Hands stuffed in his jeans pockets, he started off. A twilight glow rolled over the buildings. He should be out on the beach, where he might pick up a shot or two, but he didn't really feel like it. Something had put him in a funk.

Gradually the stores and other businesses thinned out. Last on this block was Toby's Bar and Grill. Their neon sign glowed against the darkening sky. As he passed by, the door burst open and, along with a blast of rock music, a couple stumbled out. They were laughing and talking, and the man grabbed the woman and kissed her hard.

Cody felt like an intruder. He would've walked by, but they took up most of the sidewalk. The couple broke apart, and the woman peered at him in the dim light. "Cody?"

He took a step closer. "Sylvie?" His gaze switched to the man. "Ben?"

"Yeah, yeah, it's Sylvie and Ben," Ben said, swaying a bit.

Sylvie's black hair was in a messy topknot and her clothing had the usual ruffles and flounces that made her seem to float when she walked, which she was doing now, drawing Ben toward Cody.

"Cody, Cody, Cody," she chirped. "You are the first to know."

"Know what?" he asked.

"That we are—" She cast a coy look at Ben.

"Getting mar-ried," they said in unison.

Cody blinked. "Getting married?" he repeated dumbly. "You two?"

"Yep." Ben nodded.

Sylvie held up her left hand and sure enough, an engagement ring sparkled in the neon light from the bar's sign.

"Not five minutes ago," she said, "in a cozy booth in Toby's, he proposed."

"And she said yes." Ben hiccuped.

"Well, congratulations, you two," Cody said. "I'd offer to buy you a drink, but it looks as though you've had—" He coughed and said, "Looks as though you're on your way home."

"Maybe some other time," Ben said.

"Cody, Cody, Cody."

"Yes, Sylvie?"

"I want you to take our picture. Right now. First picture of us as an engaged couple."

"Sure, I can do that." He raised his camera and looked through the eyepiece. Barely enough light, but it should work.

He snapped several shots of them kissing, of them hugging, of Sylvie holding up her ring, and one last one, which he knew would be the best—of them gazing into each other's eyes.

"I'll get these to you soon," he said, when they ran out of steam and stopped posing. "When's the date?"

"The date?" Ben frowned.

"Your wedding date. When you say the 'I dos.'"

"Oh, yeah, that. We haven't decided yet. One step at a time."

With a "see you later," they headed off. Cody continued in the opposite direction. He shook his head. They were getting married? Already? They couldn't have met more than, what, a few weeks ago. How did they know they wanted to spend the rest of their lives together?

Then he remembered what one of his buddies at the U had said. "When you meet the right person, you just know." Hmm. That sounded nuts to him, but he couldn't even imagine being in a relationship right now. He still had things to do that were best done alone.

Luci's image popped into his mind. He saw them driving out to Pine Lake together and sitting at his place, working on the article. And it dawned on him that maybe one of the reasons he was so restless tonight was because he missed her.

What was the matter with him? He and Luci could never get together. Not that way. They were miles apart in what they wanted and how they chose to live their lives.

He had to admit, though, that Ben and Sylvie looked happy. And he didn't think it was just the liquor, either.

"THE POSTERS FOR the sand-castle contest are here." Luci nodded at the stack on her desk. "And I want you to take them around."

"Me?" Tessa said. "Why?"

"Because you are my assistant, and I have other things to do today."

"Isn't there someone else who can deliver them? I'm not finished with the files."

Luci closed her eyes and took a deep breath. "I really need you to take charge of the posters, Tessa."

Tessa shuffled her flip-flops. "But can't I do something more important? Delivering them will take only a couple hours."

"Good. That sounds very efficient."

Then Luci noticed Tessa's wrinkled forehead and worried eyes, and realized that underneath her defiance lay fear. Gentling her voice, she said, "You can do this, Tessa. I know you can, or I wouldn't give you the job. Come on, I'll help you pack up, and then we'll go over the list of who gets a poster."

After Tessa left, Luci sat at her desk, savoring the silence. She'd been following Eva's advice by trying to give Tessa more responsibility, but the young woman continued to present a challenge.

Now that Luci had the office to herself, she could get some work done. Pulling up the article on Pine Lake, she read it yet again. A little tweaking here and there and it would be ready to send to the *Coastal Living* editor.

She was deep into her work when she heard "I'm b-a-a-ck." Tessa strode into the office. "All done," she said in a cheerful voice.

"Everything go well?"

"I was amazing. You'd have been proud."

"I'm sure I would have."

Tessa sighed and her mouth turned down. "So now I gotta be file drudge again."

Luci closed her eyes and took a deep breath. Patience, must have patience. She could do this. She *must* do this. This was her job.

CHAPTER TWELVE

LUCI STOOD ON the beach surveying the crowd. Sand castles were already popping up here and there. The weather had turned out as perfect as Luci had hoped, the sky cloudless, just right for Cody's picture taking.

"We'll start with the kids' contest," she said.

Cody frowned. "I would have said adults, but okay, you're the boss. Are you sure you want to leave Tessa in charge of the booth while we're gone?"

Tessa was perched on a stool, her head bent over her phone. Texting Carl, no doubt. "Marge will be here soon, and Jimmy will come by, too." Jimmy was a local high school student who did odd jobs for the chamber.

Since the day Tessa distributed the posters, Luci had been giving her more responsibility, hoping to boost her self-confidence. A risk, she knew, but one she'd decided to take.

She and Cody hadn't gone far when Hannah ran up to them and grabbed Luci's hand. "Auntie Luci, Cody, come look at our castle."

"Is it finished already?" Luci crouched to fix her niece's twisted overalls strap as Hannah practically jogged on the spot, despite her tall rubber boots.

"No, but come look. Take our picture, Cody."

"You bet." Cody grasped Hannah's free hand. "That's what I'm here for."

Hannah led them down the beach to where Spencer and Betsy, also wearing rubber boots, were intent on shaping their sand castle. An array of buckets and shovels was spread out around them, as well as piles of displaced sand. Hannah dropped Luci's and Cody's hands and ran to join her brother and her cousin.

Spencer waved at them with sand-encrusted hands. "This is fun. 'Specially 'cause I'm the boss."

Betsy wrinkled her nose. "You're always boss. But it's still fun."

"Your castle is really elaborate," Luci said. "Look at all those turrets."

"And we have a flag for the top." Betsy

held up a small red-and-white flag attached to a stick.

"Mom made the plans for us." Spencer pointed to a piece of paper lying nearby, the corners anchored to the sand with seashells.

"I found them in a library book," Arliss said from her spot on a blanket nearby.

Cody stopped and aimed his camera. "Smile pretty, Arliss."

"Don't take my picture." Arliss thrust her hands in front of her face. "I'm a mess today. Didn't have time to do more than lipstick."

"You're gorgeous," Cody said as he took the photo. "But, okay, I'll concentrate on the castle builders."

Luci looked around. "Where's Don? And Will and Francine? And Megan? I thought this was a family effort?"

"Don and Will took Megan to get something to drink," Arliss said. "The other kids were giving her a bad time." She sighed. "They all started out okay, and then suddenly there were tears."

"Where's Francine?"

"You need to ask?" Arliss pursed her lips. "Saturday is her best selling day—along with Sunday, and Monday through Friday. Don't get me wrong. I love taking care of the kids, but her job's running away with her, if you ask me. Which no one does."

"Mom and Dad coming later?" Luci asked.

"Should be here anytime."

"Are Don and Dad still on the outs? I've asked Mom a couple of times, but she never answers my question."

Arliss laughed. "Typical Anna. Much as I love my mother-in-law, she's good at avoiding questions that make her uncomfortable. But, yes, Don and Erv are still having problems. They have to speak to each other at the bank, but who knows how long that will last?"

Luci would have asked more, but just then, Don, Will and Megan returned. Don carried two cups of coffee. Will, wearing his Jackson's Boat Works cap, held his coffee in one hand and clasped Megan's hand with the other. She trudged along, head bent, clutching a can of soda to her chest.

"Hey, you two," Will said. He tugged Megan's hand. "Say hi to your aunt and Cody."

"Hi," Megan mumbled into her can of soda.

Will shrugged and shook his head.

Don greeted Luci and Cody. He handed

Arliss her coffee and then put his arm around Luci's shoulders. "Look at you, Miss Important Person. Or is he the one I should bow down to?"

"It's a joint effort," Cody said.

Luci raised her eyebrows. "Uh-uh. Truth is, we pretty much do our own thing and if we're lucky, we can put something together and call it a project."

"Aw, now, Luci," Cody began. "I'm not that hard to work with."

"Okay, you two," Don said. "Time out. We've got some kids here who want their pictures taken. Right, kiddos?" He focused on the children clustered around the sand castle.

"And now that Megan's here, we'll get some pictures," Cody said.

Will gave Megan's shoulders a gentle nudge. "Go sit with the other kids, Meggie."

Megan pushed out her lower lip. "No."

"Come on, honey," Arliss said. "Cody wants to take your picture."

"I don't care."

Cody went over to Megan and knelt beside her. "Want to see some of my pictures?" He held out his camera.

Megan squeezed her eyes shut. "No."

"I have one of you. Right here." He tapped the camera's screen.

Megan opened one eye. "You do?"

"Yep. I took it a few minutes ago when you were running to catch up with your dad." He held the camera closer.

"Wow." Her face lit up. "Is that me?"

Arliss leaned over to look, too. "It is. What a beautiful picture."

"Would you like to have it?" Cody asked.

"Maybe." Megan eyed him cautiously.

"It's yours, but I need one of you with the others while you're working on the sand castle. Then Auntie Luci will put both pictures in pretty folders and you can have them."

"I don't want a picture of them." She turned away from the other children.

"Your parents really want one of all of you. Can we make a deal? What if the picture of you by yourself is just for you?"

"Well…okay."

Cody stood and held out his hand. Megan set her soda down and put her hand in his. When they'd joined the other children, Cody said, "Okay, kids, I'm calling a truce while we do some picture taking."

"What's a truce?" Spencer stopped shoveling sand to look up at Cody.

"That means we stop fighting and get along. Luci and I know what a truce is, don't we?" He turned to give Luci a wink.

"We do," Luci said with an exaggerated nod.

"So, do I have your cooperation?"

"I guess so," Spencer grumbled. "But she didn't want to help before."

"Did, too!" Megan said.

Cody held up a hand. "Truce, remember?"

"She can help dig the moat," Spencer said, "but not the tower. That's mine."

"I don't care about your old tower," Megan said, and she picked up a shovel and knelt at the half-dug moat. Betsy and Hannah were building the wall that surrounded the castle. With all the children in place, Cody raised his camera and began taking pictures.

Luci sat beside Arliss to watch.

"He's good with kids," Arliss said, sipping her coffee.

"He is. I'd no idea. He was an only child, too."

"Must be instinctive. Whatever it is, he's got the touch. He's a keeper, Luci."

Luci shook her head. "Not for me. By the time he gets ready to settle down—if ever—I'll be old and gray."

Arliss laughed. "I don't know, you two seem pretty close to me."

"That's only 'cause we have to work together."

"No, it's more than that. I've seen the way he looks at you."

Luci drew back and raised her eyebrows. "What do you mean?"

"You know, the way a guy looks at a woman he's in love with."

Luci shook her head vigorously. "No, no. He's just a friend."

As she followed Cody down the beach to photograph the next sand castle, Luci tried to forget Arliss's words. Cody was *not* in love with her.

As though sensing her gaze on him, he turned to her. "What?"

"Just thinking how good you were with the kids. Getting them to pose. Arliss thought so, too."

He shook his head and laughed. "I've never

worked so hard in my life. I'm used to letting a picture just happen."

"Well, I'm glad you worked on that one. The family will be grateful to have the photo of all the kids together, and it will make this a really memorable occasion. And I'm betting that in years to come the kids will be thankful, too. By that time, they'll probably all be getting along famously."

She hoped.

They worked their way down the beach, Cody photographing the kids building their castles, Luci recording contact info and handing out claim tickets.

"Hey, there's Mark and Eva and the kids." Cody pointed to a group clustered around a sand-castle-in-progress.

Luci spotted the couple, along with their daughter, twelve-year-old Sasha, and their four-year-old son, Elijah. With them were the *Herald*'s advertising manager, Bernie Sanchez, his wife, Maria, and their two children. Bella was Sasha's age, and the girls were best friends. Manuel, seven, was Maria's nephew, whom they'd adopted after his parents had passed away.

Mark looked up as they approached. "Hey, good to see you're on the job."

"Are you going to take our picture?" Sasha asked. She and Bella were working on the castle's round tower. Elijah and Manuel seemed more interested in throwing globs of sand at each other.

"I sure am," Cody said.

"Then I need to wipe off Eli's face." Eva dug a tissue from her tote and, despite his protests, cleaned the sand from his cheeks. Maria did the same for Manuel.

Luci studied Eli, unable to decide whom he resembled the most. He had his mother's dark hair and deep-set eyes, but his father's wide-mouthed grin. Either way, he was a cute kid.

While Cody took the kids' pictures, Bernie said, "This is like old times, seeing you two working together."

"Not quite," Luci said. "At the *Herald*, Eva and Mark were the bosses."

Cody lowered his camera between shots. "And now she thinks she's the boss." His eyes flashed as he tipped his head toward Luci.

She stuck her hand on her hip. "I *am* the boss."

Cody backed up. "Whatever you say." He winked at the others.

Luci shook her head. "He's almost as bad as my other assistant."

"Assistant? You have an assistant?" Mark handed a shovel to Elijah.

"Yep. Eva's already heard about her." She filled the others in on Tessa and her attitude, hoping her friends might have some advice.

"We can relate," Mark said. "We had someone at the *Herald* a few years ago who caused trouble."

"Remember April?" Eva asked.

Luci and Cody both nodded.

"Did she want your job?" Luci asked.

Eva laughed. "Not exactly. She wanted Mark."

Mark shrugged and grinned. "Hey, what can I say? I can't help that women find me irresistible."

"You wish." Eva gave him a soft punch on the shoulder.

"You have to watch these men," Maria said. "A little female attention goes to their heads."

"Aw, throw us a bone now and then, why

don'cha?" Bernie raised both hands in a begging position.

They all laughed.

"THOSE WERE GOOD TIMES," Cody said as he and Luci continued down the beach. "When we were both at the *Herald*."

"They were." Luci stepped aside to dodge a group of kids running by. "Your encouragement meant a lot to me."

"Glad I could help."

She glanced at him and their gazes collided. His smile faded, and for a moment he looked as though he wanted to say something else. Something serious.

Then the moment passed. He gave her a pat on the shoulder and said, "Yep, those were good times."

CHAPTER THIRTEEN

AFTER THEY FINISHED photographing the children's contest, Luci and Cody ventured into the adults' territory. Here the sand castles tended to be more elaborate, with many of the contestants following professional-looking blueprints. But the adults seemed just as pleased as the kids to have their photos taken, and Luci was busy handing out claim checks.

"Hey, there's Sylvie and Ben." Cody pointed toward a couple busy constructing a castle.

"So, they're still together."

Cody gave a short laugh. "More than that—they're getting married."

Luci stopped and stared. "What?"

"I ran into them the other night, just after he popped the question—in Toby's Bar and Grill."

"How romantic."

"She thought it was," Cody said. "She was

bubbling over. 'Course they'd both had a few. C'mon, we'll do them next. You can get the scoop."

They trudged through the sand and the streaming crowds, and reached the couple.

"Hey, Ben, Sylvie," Cody said from behind his camera. They looked up and Cody snapped a shot. "Gotcha!"

"There's Mr. Cameraman." Sylvie stood and pushed back hair that had escaped her topknot. "You'd better take another one, though. I think I have sand on my nose."

"No, but you do now." Ben scooped up a handful of sand and came at Sylvie.

She put up both hands to ward him off. "Don't you dare mess me up."

He stopped and let the sand filter through his fingers. "Okay, but it'll cost you."

Her eyes widened, and she looked back and forth from him to Cody and Luci. "Not in front of them."

"Go ahead." Cody aimed his camera again.

Ben wiped his hands on his jeans and grabbed Sylvie by the shoulders. Their kiss was so full of love and affection that Luci couldn't help sighing. Not that she lamented the loss of Ben. But their happiness made her heart ache for someone special, too.

"Congratulations on your engagement," she said when they'd finally broken apart.

"Thanks." Sylvie beamed. "I wish I could show you my ring, but I didn't want to get sand in it."

"I told her she could wear gloves," Ben said. "But she said no."

"I've been doing this sand-castle thing since I was a kid," Sylvie said. "Your hands have to be bare to get the full effect. I hated to take off my ring, though."

Luci filled out a claim check for the photos and handed it to Ben. "When is the big day?"

"We're not sure yet, but soon." Ben tucked the slip of paper into his shirt pocket.

"It won't be a large wedding," Sylvie said. "But of course you're invited. We wouldn't have met without you two."

"Oh, I expect in a small town like Willow Beach you would have met sooner or later," Luci said.

"I'm glad it was sooner." Sylvie laughed. "I was beginning to think I'd be single forever."

Luci and Cody said their goodbyes and

headed for the next group of contestants. "I'm happy for them," Luci said.

"I hope it works out."

"You sound doubtful."

He shrugged. "They're so different. She's off-the-wall and he's—"

"By the book."

Cody laughed. "Yeah, that describes him."

"You know the old saying about opposites attracting."

"I know, but having something in common is important, too."

"You think? Okay, take me for example. What would someone have to have in common with me?"

Cody nodded. "Easy. Roots. And not just anywhere—but here in Willow Beach. And he'd have to want a family."

"Wait a minute. I don't ever remember telling you I wanted kids."

"You didn't have to. Family is so important to you, it's only logical that you want your own. That's a no-brainer."

"Okay, okay." She made a dismissive wave. "What else?"

He stopped and studied her. She held her breath as she waited for him to speak.

He stroked his chin. "Hmm. Okay, a keen mind. An appreciation of the written word. A sense of humor."

"Now we're getting to the good stuff."

"Oh, there's lots of good stuff, Luci. You'll make some lucky guy a great wife and partner."

Luci bit her lip and turned away. "We'd better start printing the photos. People will be wanting to pick them up soon."

On the way back to the booth, they passed Luci's family again. "Wow, look at the progress they've made," she said. The moat was finished and the castle had two towers, the tallest at least three feet high.

"Your parents are there now," Cody said. "And who else?" He peered ahead.

"I don't know. Looks like she's got a child with her, though. She could be the boy's grandmother."

"Uh-oh," Cody said.

"What?" she asked. "Do you know them?"

Cody kept his gaze lowered as he fussed with his camera. "Ah, I may have seen them around."

"Let's go over. I want to say hi to Mom and Dad, anyway."

"Do we have time?"

"We won't take long." When he still didn't move, she asked, "What's wrong?"

"Nothing, nothing. I'll go.'

When they reached the group, Spencer, Betsy and Hannah were putting the finishing touches on the sand castle.

Betsy waved her shovel. "Look, Auntie Luci. We're almost done."

"I see," Luci said. "Your castle is beautiful."

"The judges came by." Spencer brushed his hands together to shake off the sand. "And I could tell they really liked it."

"I bet we win," Hannah chimed in.

"You do, and I'll be taking your picture again," Cody warned.

"Oh, goodie!" Hannah jumped up and down.

Will and Don were deep in conversation, probably about boats. Don's interest in boats had given him a relationship with his brother-in-law that he didn't have anymore with his father.

Speaking of their father, where was he? Looking around, she saw him near the shore. Head down, hands shoved in his pockets, he paced a circle in the sand. Luci took a moment to wonder at her father's odd behavior, but then her gaze moved on to where Anna and Arliss, who held Megan's hand, were talking to the newcomer. The little boy, a cute kid a bit younger than Megan, ran in circles, flapping his arms and making sounds like an airplane.

Anna beckoned to Luci and Cody. "This is Helen Stevens," she said when the two joined them. "She's visiting from—where did you say? California?"

"Yes," Helen said. "LA."

"This is my youngest daughter, Luci, and her, ah, friend? Associate? I don't know what to call you, Cody." Anna laughed.

"All of the above," Cody said. "Hi, Ms. Stevens."

"Call me Helen. Both of you. Please. Nice to see you again, Cody."

"So you do know each other," Luci said. Why hadn't Cody mentioned that when they'd first spotted the woman?

"We, ah…" Cody began.

"Met in Oceanside." Helen rested both hands on her cane. "At the kids' park."

"Right," Cody said. "I stopped there on my way back from the campground."

"And Jason and I were there because Jason's been begging me to go on the rides ever since we arrived." She beckoned to the boy. "Jason, come over here and meet Luci."

Arms still stretched out, Jason ran to them.

"Okay, enough already." Helen captured him and pulled him to her side. "This is Luci. She's aunt to Spencer, Betsy, Hannah and Megan."

"Wow," Luci said. "You know all the children's names already."

"Oh, yes," Helen said.

Jason looked up at Cody. "Hi, I remember you." He turned to Luci and held out his hand. "Pleased to meet you." His smile revealed a missing front tooth.

Luci leaned over to shake his hand. "How old are you, Jason?"

"Six."

"Why, you're close to Megan's age. Did you build a sand castle today?"

"Uh-uh." Jason dug the toe of his shoe into the sand.

"We didn't know about the contest in time," Helen said, smoothing Jason's cowlick.

"You're visiting? Or did you move here?"

"Visiting. We're staying with a friend in Oceanside."

"Megan, honey," Arliss said, "why don't you show Jason the shells you found?"

Before Megan could reply, Helen said, "We'd better be on our way. Maybe next time we see you, the children can get better acquainted."

Luci thought that an odd remark. How did Helen know there would be a next time? Oceanside wasn't that far away, but it wasn't Willow Beach, either.

Helen leaned heavily on her cane as she and Jason walked down the beach.

"I wonder what's wrong with her," Luci said.

"I don't know," Anna replied. "She seems nice. And her grandson, too."

"She looked sad," Arliss said. "And older than she probably is. I think she was very beautiful, once. Her eyes are expressive."

"What did you think of her, Cody?" Luci asked. He'd hardly said a word to Helen. Ordinarily, that would have been because he was busy taking pictures, but he wasn't doing that, either.

"I, ah, why are you asking me?"

"You've known her longer than all of us. But, oh, never mind. We need to get back to the tent. I'll say hi to Dad and we'll be on our way." She turned to her mother. "Is he okay? Why is he over there all by himself?"

Anna shook her head. "He's got a lot on his mind. But don't ask me what. Sometimes, I feel like I don't know that man at all, even after thirty-five years of marriage."

While Cody joined Will and Don, Luci walked over to her father. He'd stopped pacing and stood with his back to the others, arms folded, staring at the ocean.

"What do you think of the contest?" she asked.

He shrugged. "You'd be the best judge of that, considering it's your project."

She studied him. "Are you okay, Dad? You look a little, I don't know, tired or something."

"I'm okay."

He smiled, but his eyes were sad, like Helen Stevens's eyes.

"Maybe you and Mom should take a vacation, go somewhere fun. How long has it been since you've gone somewhere by your-selves?"

Before he could reply, Anna joined them. "Erv, you barely said anything to Helen Stevens. She probably thought you were rude, walking off like you did."

"We'd better go," Erv said. "We've got some more people to talk to."

"You go on," Anna said. "I want to stay here and see how the kids finish their castle. You can talk to your cronies without me."

Erv frowned.

"Go on, now." Anna shooed him away.

"All right." He grumbled under his breath and then stalked off down the beach.

Anna pursed her lips and shook her head. "He wants to catch up with Bud and Jim and brag about his below-par golf score."

"That is something to brag about."

"And he complains that all I want to do is talk to my garden club friends." Anna sighed. "Sometimes, I wonder how we ever got to-gether."

Luci put her arm around her mother's shoulders. "I don't know, but I'm sure glad you did."

Anna leaned her head on Luci's shoulder.

"Yes, honey, so am I. I wouldn't trade you kids—or my grandkids—for anything."

But what about Dad? Luci wanted to ask. Did her mom want to trade him?

"WHERE'S THE REST of the photo paper?" Cody asked. "I'm nearly out and we still have a few dozen pictures to process."

He was pleased with how the photos were turning out and judging by the comments they'd been getting, the recipients were happy, too. But that could change if he and Luci had to start turning people away.

"Is there more paper in that box?" Luci stopped sorting folders and pointed to a box under the table.

"Nope. I already checked."

"I made a list of supplies for Tessa to pack up," Luci said. "I'm sure I included enough paper. Let's see, the list is around here some-where. Oh, here is it." She picked up a sheet of paper and ran her finger down the page. "Paper, eight packs."

"We didn't have eight packs. Tessa must have messed up."

Luci put down the list and sighed. "And now she's gone. Jimmy, too."

Luci had let both kids go shortly after she and Cody returned to the tent. They were eager to leave, and Cody couldn't blame them. They deserved to have some fun after hanging out in the tent for most of the day.

"I'll run back to the chamber and get some more paper," Luci said, "while you stay here and keep working."

"I hate to have you do that."

"It's not that far and it won't take long. I'd better get going, though. All we need is for Glen to show up and find people waiting for their photos."

Cody loaded the last of the paper into the printer. "Where's he been all day?"

"I saw him a couple times, out and about." Luci hooked her purse strap over her shoulder. "Busy being chamber president. Back soon." She stepped onto the path leading through the dunes.

A COUPLE APPEARED, eager to claim their photo, and Cody took care of them. After that, several more people showed up, which kept the printer humming.

When there was a lull in activity, he checked the time. Luci should be back by now, unless she'd run into trouble. He ducked out from under the tent and walked along the path. No Luci here. Seeing no customers at the chamber's tent, he went a few steps farther.

Ever since he'd seen Helen and Jason with Luci's family, Cody had been fighting an internal war. Luci seemed to accept his account of how he'd met Helen, but didn't she wonder exactly how—or why—they had struck up a conversation? What if she asked him about that meeting? What would he say? *Oh, yeah, I recognized Helen as the woman your father was having a heated conversation with in a coffee shop.*

Luci was his friend—more than a friend—and he didn't want to hurt her.

While he stood there debating the issue, he glimpsed her walking along the sidewalk. She wore a backpack, no doubt full of photo paper. When she saw him, Luci smiled and waved.

"I was coming to see what happened to you," he said. "Here, let me take that."

"Okay." She waited while he lifted the pack from her back.

He slung the straps over one shoulder. "What took you so long?"

"When I got to the office, I couldn't find my key to the supply room. It's supposed to be in my desk, but apparently Tessa forgot to put it back after she used it. I finally found Marge's key. Why did you leave the booth?"

"There was a break in customers. I was worried about you."

"We'd better get back in case someone's waiting."

When they reached the booth, Cody dumped the backpack onto the table just as a boy of about ten ran under the tent. He waved his claim ticket. "Are the pictures done? Are the pictures done?"

Behind him came his parents, holding hands with a toddler. "Georgie wants to see them, too," the boy said, ruffling his brother's hair.

Luci took the child's ticket and checked it off on her list. "We'll have your picture for you in just a few minutes. While Cody's printing it, you can pick out the folder you'd like. Here are the samples." The family gathered around to look.

After they left, more people arrived to

keep Cody busy. Still, he was afraid that the issue of Helen and Erv wasn't going away anytime soon.

CHAPTER FOURTEEN

"THAT'S THE LAST CUSTOMER." Luci watched the family they had just waited on leave the tent and head down the beach.

Cody switched off the printer. "Yep, time to head out."

While he packed up the equipment, Lucy put the leftover folders and coupon books into a box. All around them, the occupants of the other tents were also getting ready to leave, and the sounds of people calling out and trucks backing up filled the air.

"Are you staying for the barbecue and bonfire?" she asked, not sure what to do with herself now their job was over.

Cody shrugged and tucked a lens into his leather camera bag. "I don't know. Hadn't thought much about it."

"I can smell the barbecue already." She nodded toward the beach, where half-a-dozen grills and a row of tables were set up. A little farther on, people had gathered driftwood for a bonfire.

Cody lifted his head and sniffed the air. "That smells too good pass up. Let's do it."

"I wasn't angling for an invitation. I was just curious if you were staying or not."

"So, do you have other plans?"

Oh, how she wished she could say yes. She really needed to do something about her social life. Or lack of it. "No," she said. "Do you?"

"If I did, I wouldn't be suggesting we hang out together. Shall we?"

"Okay…sure."

As soon as the workers drove off with the tent and other equipment, Luci and Cody joined the crowd gathered around the barbecues. They took their hotdogs, bags of chips and cans of soda to one of the tables. As they chatted with their tablemates, Luci relaxed. But, when they finished eating, her nerves knotted again.

"Now what?" she asked him.

He shrugged. "You want to walk around for a while, see who's here?"

"Why not?"

They mingled with the crowd, stopping

here and there to chat with people they knew. After spending a few minutes talking to a couple she'd known in high school, Luci turned to find Cody gone. She finally spotted him with Max Billings and his wife. She was about to join them but then worried that Cody would think she was being too clingy.

As she stood there debating what to do, Cody tossed back his head and laughed at something Max said. One of Max's employees whispered something in Cody's ear. He laughed again and placed a hand on her shoulder.

Luci's stomach sank.

Stop thinking about him. Let him go.

How many times had she given herself that lecture over the past few years? What was wrong with her? Why couldn't she accept the truth about their relationship and move on?

She walked down the beach, continuing to greet people she knew, laughing and talking as though she was having a good time. She was, wasn't she?

The sun slid toward the horizon, the perfect end to a perfect day. Of course, Cody would photograph the event. She wondered how many photos he had of Willow Beach sunsets. Probably hundreds. Yep, there he was, aiming his camera at orange and red rays spread along the horizon.

As soon as the sun disappeared, someone lit the bonfire. The crowd cheered and gathered around the fledgling flames.

She looked around for Cody but didn't see him. Now that the sunset was over, he'd probably gone home.

Maybe she could join her family. That was where she belonged, anyway. However, she didn't see them anywhere. That was odd. She would've thought they'd all be gathered around the fire.

Okay, time for her to go home. She trudged through the sand toward the sidewalk that led into town. Some of the stores would still be open. Maybe she'd stop somewhere for a cup of tea.

She'd almost reached the sidewalk when someone called her name. She turned around to see Cody running toward her. He carried a rolled-up blanket under his arm.

"Not going home, are you? Already?"

"I don't know," she said. "Maybe. Why?"

"Don't you want to sit by the bonfire? They're going to have a sing-along."

"When I didn't see you around anywhere I thought you'd left." Luci bit her lip, grateful that her blush wouldn't be visible in the dim light.

"I went to my car to get this—" he held up the blanket "—for us to sit on."

"Well…"

"Come on. The bonfire is part of the sand-castle-contest experience. You worked hard today. Relax for a while." He held out his hand.

She put her hand in his, and they walked back to the beach.

The bonfire roared and crackled, sending sparks into the air and lighting the faces of the onlookers. They sat on the blanket with their backs against a log, apart from the group but close enough to feel the fire's warmth. A man and a woman with guitars slung over their shoulders entertained the crowd.

"They're good," Luci said.

Cody nodded. "They play at Toby's."

"Oh, is that one of your hangouts now?" she teased.

"I stop in now and then for a beer. That's

where I ran into Sylvie and Ben, the night he proposed."

"I saw them somewhere around here." Luci straightened and peered into the semidarkness.

"Yeah, they're over there."

Sure enough, they were huddled together, their arms around each other. They faced the fire, smiling, eyes glowing in the firelight. When the song ended, Ben cupped Sylvie's cheek, turned her face to his and kissed her. Luci squeezed her eyes shut and imagined she was kissing someone with such…such what? *Come on, wordsmith.* With such fervor, with such…love. Cody was watching the couple, too.

"They've got it bad," he said, shaking his head.

"But isn't that a good thing?" She elbowed him in the side.

He caught her hand. "Hey, that's my soft spot."

"You have a soft spot?"

"'Course, I do. Everyone has one."

She expected him to let go of her hand, but he didn't. She settled back against the log and thought how good her hand felt in his. Secure, connected.

The players strummed their guitars, preparing for another song. "Y'all join in," the man said.

They played the introductory chords to a familiar love song. Luci knew the words and sang along. Cody joined in, too.

He was still holding her hand and before she knew it, she was leaning against his shoulder. And then he put his arm around her. She closed her eyes and rested against him.

After the song was over, she expected him to take his arm away, but he didn't, so she nestled even closer. They didn't say much, just listened to the music, singing along when they knew the words, watching the fire slowly die down.

After a while, stars bright in the sky, the waves softly breaking on the shore, people began folding up their blankets and drifting away. Here and there, a goodbye or a "see ya" rang out.

"Maybe we should go, too," Cody said.

"I guess." She didn't want to move. She was way too comfortable.

Cody eased his arm from around her shoulders and steadied her as she sat up. "I'll take you back to your apartment."

Luci brushed sand from her blouse. "I can walk."

"In the dark, by yourself? No way."

She smiled. "Willow Beach is a safe place. I'm not afraid."

"Are you saying you don't want my company?"

"Oh, no. I just don't want you to feel obligated, that's all."

"Sometimes, obligation is a good thing," he said.

She thought about pursuing that, but before she could, he stood and held out his hand. She allowed him to pull her to her feet. They folded the blanket and walked to the lot where his SUV was parked.

The ride to her apartment was all too short. She thought about inviting him in, but her better sense said no, let him go.

However, he insisted on coming around and helping her from the SUV.

"Always the gentleman," she said as she stepped to the ground.

"I've got to be good for something."

He walked her to her door. As she turned

to say good-night, he placed his hands on her shoulders.

"Thanks for all you did today," Luci said. "You made the contest special for so many people."

"As long as we're passing out compliments, so did you."

He stepped nearer. She knew he intended to kiss her cheek, as he often did. As brief as a blink, he would brush his lips against her skin and leave her feeling as though she'd had only one bite of a cookie before it was snatched away.

But this time, his lips landed on her lips. His eyes widened and then closed as he settled his mouth more firmly on hers. His arms slipped from her shoulders and captured her waist, drawing her against him in a warm embrace. Seizing the moment, she wrapped her arms around his neck and gave herself up to the kiss.

At last, with a soft sigh, he drew away. Not knowing what to say, she waited for him to speak first.

Finally, he eased his arms from around her and took her hands in both of his. "Shouldn't have done that," he said in a low voice.

Her heart sank. That wasn't what she'd wanted to hear. "But you did. We did."

"I know. And that's all I'll say about it. Good night, Luci."

"Good night, Cody."

Inside her apartment, Luci peeked through the curtains to watch Cody wheel his car around and drive from the cul-de-sac. Then she turned away. The kiss hadn't changed anything between them. But, then, why should it? He still had the world to explore while her little world was right here in Willow Beach.

CHAPTER FIFTEEN

LUCI PULLED HER car into her parents' driveway. She turned off the ignition but didn't unbuckle her seat belt. Considering how disastrous the previous Sundays had been, she'd hesitated to come today. However, she hadn't heard that dinner was canceled, so here she was. But where were the others?

"Hello!" she called as she stepped inside the house. Instead of the sounds of children playing, silence greeted her. No one was in the living room or on the porch. She continued on to the kitchen, where she expected to find her mother bustling about as usual, preparing dinner. Ready to help, she rolled up her sleeves and pushed through the swinging doors.

Anna sat at the kitchen table staring into space.

Luci hurried to her side. "Mom, what's wrong?"

Her mother looked up and gave a weak smile. "Hello, dear." She pulled a tissue from her pocket and swiped at her eyes, which were red rimmed.

"You've been crying. What's the matter? Are you sick?" Luci sat next to Anna and put an arm around her shoulders.

"No, I'm fine."

"You're not fine, and I want to know what's wrong."

Her mother pushed back her chair and stood, slipping from under Luci's arm. "I'd better get the gravy made. The chicken will be done soon."

"I can do the gravy."

Her mother pressed her lips together and shook her head. "No, no, my job."

"I'll check on the chicken." Luci crossed to the stove and opened the oven door. She pulled out the pan, picked up a spoon and basted the roasting chicken. "Mmm, smells delicious."

Anna made no response as she took out measuring spoons from a drawer and then pulled the lid from a canister of flour.

Luci returned the chicken to the oven and shut the door. "Where is everyone?"

"Don's fishing with Max."

"On a Sunday?"

"Something about the tides. I don't know. Spencer has a stomachache, so Arliss decided to keep both kids home. Will took Betsy and Megan to the movies."

"Instead of coming here?"

Anna shrugged. "It was the last day of a film they just had to see." She moved to the stove and poured the flour into a skillet. "Francine's doing her usual." She gave Luci an apologetic look. "I should have called and told you not to come."

"No, no, I want to be here. We can have a nice dinner, just the three of us. Been a long time since I've had my parents to myself. Dad's working in his study, right?"

"I suppose so."

"Mom, is Dad okay? He hasn't seemed himself lately."

"I wouldn't know." Anna stirred the gravy so hard that some of it sloshed over the side of the pot.

Luci frowned. "You know Dad better than anyone."

"Do I? I don't think so."

"Mom, what's going on?"

"Could you steam the broccoli, dear? I forgot all about it."

When dinner was ready, Luci knocked on the door to her father's study. Instead of his usual "Come in," he opened the door and peered out. "Oh, it's you," he said, instead of his usual "Hello, youngest," or "How's my girl?"

The three of them sat at the table, her father at one end, her mother at the other and Luci in the middle. She tried to make conversation, mostly about the sand-castle contest, but her remarks were met with "That's nice, dear" from her mother and nods from her father.

They were eating their ice cream when Francine arrived. She filled a plate with leftovers and joined them at the table. Luci expected the conversation to pick up, but it didn't. She made a few more attempts and then gave up.

Afterward, Erv retreated to his study again. Anna insisted on cleaning up the kitchen by herself. "You two girls spend some time together," she said. "Catch up on your news."

"All right." Francine motioned to Luci. "Come on, let's go outside."

After the heavy atmosphere of the house, the backyard offered a refreshing change. Luci took a deep breath of the ocean air and followed Francine across the lawn to Anna's gardens, where they stopped to admire the roses.

"Good to see you today, Fran," Luci said and meant it. She'd missed her sister this summer. Although they were six years apart, they'd had some good times together while growing up.

Francine bent to smell a cluster of roses. "I know I haven't been around much, but I've been really busy."

"You work hard."

Francine straightened and tucked a lock of hair back into the twist at her nape. "I have to. Will's hours were cut."

"Oh, I didn't know."

Francine shrugged. "I'm thankful Arliss can take care of the girls. She's a good mother. Better than me." She bit her lip and looked away.

Luci didn't know what to say, but before she could think of something, Fran said, "What about you? Have you found the perfect job, like you wanted?"

"Ah, too early to say. Ask me again at the end of the summer."

They walked a little farther and then stopped at a different part of the garden. "Fran, do you know what's going on with Mom and Dad?

Francine frowned. "What are you talking about?"

"When I arrived today, Mom had been crying. And Dad's hiding out in his office most of the time."

Francine waved a hand. "She's probably upset because her roses didn't win any ribbons at the flower show this year. Having her flowers ignored always upsets her. She puts her heart and soul into this garden. And Dad's always working. Nothing new there. He drummed a strong work ethic into us from the time we were old enough to earn an allowance."

"I hear what you're saying, but I think there's something more going on."

Francine's phone chimed. She dug it out of her jacket pocket and looked at the screen. "I need to take this." She pressed the phone to her ear and stepped away. "Really? Ready to make an offer? I'll be right there."

Fran ended the call, a wide grin on her face. "Gotta run, Luce. Hot prospect finally steps up to the plate. See you later."

"Okay, see you…later." Whenever that would be. Given Fran's work schedule, probably not anytime soon.

After Fran left, Luci wandered to the edge of the yard and sat on one of the wrought-iron benches facing the ocean. The white-capped waves and dark clouds meant a storm was brewing. Near the horizon, a freighter chugged to Canada, while fishing boats from all directions converged into a V as they approached the inlet leading to the marina.

She sat there trying to remember the warmth and security that belonging to her family had always provided.

Would her family ever recover the happiness and harmony of the past? Or had they already reached the point of no return?

CHAPTER SIXTEEN

"Where do you want this mirror hung?" Cody asked. Today wasn't a major redecorate-the-house day, just a minimove, where one or two items were added or taken away or simply shifted from one spot to another.

Glass cleaner and cloth in hand, Olive came to stand beside him. She gazed at the oval, gilt-framed mirror leaning against the living room wall. "I don't know. I'd thought in the entryway, above the table against the wall, but maybe it's too big for there. It doesn't go anywhere, really."

"Then why are you keeping it?"

She stepped forward and sprayed cleaner on the mirror. "Because it belonged to your great-aunt Clara. On your father's side. It's an heirloom."

"Is it valuable?"

"Not moneywise."

"Since you have no place to put it, why not take it to the shop and sell it?"

"Because it keeps me connected to Aunt Clara." Olive scrubbed the mirror with her cloth and then stepped back to view the results.

"Did you actually know her?"

"I met her once, right after Ed and I were married. I'll never forget how warm and welcoming she was. We sat in her parlor and she served us tea and little cakes she'd made."

"She sounds like a nice lady."

"She was, and when she passed away, her son asked if there was something of hers I'd like to have. I remembered seeing this mirror in her parlor, and so that's what I chose. Go ahead and hang it in the entry, and I'll find a better table to match it."

They moved a few more pieces of furniture around until Olive was satisfied, and then Cody said, "How 'bout we go catch some dinner?"

Olive wrinkled her forehead. "I, ah, already have plans."

"You and Emma having a ladies' night out?"

Olive looked away. "No…"

"What? What's the big secret?"

"I have a date." She looked at him sheepishly.

Cody took a step back and raised both hands. "Whoa, that's a surprise. I mean, not that you shouldn't, or couldn't… Okay, I'm digging myself a hole here. Why don't you just tell me about it?"

"Mel Simpson's back in town."

"The guy from Wenatchee, with the apple orchard? Is he visiting his daughter again?"

"No, he's moving here. He turned his orchard over to his son and bought one of those new houses up on the bluff."

Before Cody could ask any more questions, the doorbell rang.

"That must be Mel now." Olive hurried to the door, pausing in front of the mirror to pat her hair. "Oh, I look a mess."

"You look fine, Mom."

Olive opened the door. "Come in, Mel."

A tall, husky dude with a gray crew cut, Mel Simpson looked ready for an evening out. He was wearing a long-sleeved dress shirt and neatly pressed slacks.

Olive took his hand and drew him toward Cody. "You remember my son."

"Sure do." Mel's smile was wide as he extended his free hand. "How're you doing?"

"Good. Good." Cody shook Mel's hand, still adjusting to this turn of events.

"You're early," Olive said. "I'm not ready."

"Thought you might need help moving stuff." Mel glanced around. "I see you got the mirror hung."

"Cody dropped by to help me."

Cody folded his arms and rocked back on his heels. "Yep. We've got everything under control."

"Just give me a few minutes, Mel."

Mel waved a hand. "Don't hurry. Plenty of time till our reservation."

"Could you get Mel a beer?" Olive asked.

"You have beer?" His mother didn't drink often and when she did, she preferred wine.

"Mel brought it over," Olive said.

Mel was already stocking her refrigerator? This was looking serious.

Cody and Mel took their beers out to the front porch and sat in wicker chairs. The house was several blocks from the ocean but elevated enough to afford a pretty good view. The water looked calm today, and the sky was a soft blue.

"Mom says you're moving here," Cody said.

Mel nodded. "Yep. Turned over the orchard to Harold—he's my son. 'Course we'll go back at harvest time. Don't want to miss that."

"We? Uh, you and your daughter?"

"No. Me and Olive. Can't wait to show her my spread." Mel leaned back and propped his ankle on his knee.

"And she knows she's going."

Mel gave him a curious look. "'Course she does. You should come, too."

"Thanks, but I don't know where I'll be then. I'm waiting for my next job."

"That's right—Olive says you travel a lot." Mel sipped his beer and asked Cody about some of the trips he'd been on, which carried the conversation until Olive arrived.

As she stepped out the door, Mel widened his eyes and gave a low whistle. "You are one gorgeous gal."

Olive blushed. "Thought I'd better dress up a little."

She smoothed the skirt of a dress Cody hadn't seen her wear since her friend's granddaughter's christening.

"Big night on the town?" Cody asked.

"Dinner at the Beach Café," Olive said, "and then we're going to the play at the Little Theater. They're doing *Sound of Music*."

"I see," Cody said. "Well, you kids have fun."

"We will," Olive said.

"We always do," Mel added. He held out his hand to Olive. "C'mon, Miss Gorgeous. Let's do it."

CODY DROVE ALONG the Coast Highway, his thoughts on tonight's surprise visitor. He didn't resent Mel taking an interest in his mother. Not at all. He often wished she'd find someone special and now that it appeared she had, he couldn't be happier for her. But he needed some time to get used to the idea. Going on one of his getaways would help. He always escaped when he had trouble coping with something. When he thought about it, maybe traveling the world as a freelance photographer was, in essence, just one big escape.

Life was so much simpler when he was on assignment. Look how complicated things were already, after little more than a month in Willow Beach. Besides his mother's new situation, and the possibility that she'd marry Mel and move away, he'd become involved in whatever Erv and Helen had going on.

And then there was Luci. He was pretty sure she still had a crush on him, and he honestly didn't know how he felt about her. Last night's kiss had played over and over in his mind. He'd intended to give her the usual kiss on her cheek, but somehow he'd kissed her on the lips instead. The sensation of her warm mouth melding with his had sent him reeling.

He spotted a side road leading to the ocean and, on just the kind of impulse he relished, took the turn. He passed an RV park, where campers were enjoying their escape from the city, and continued on to where the pavement ended at the dunes. He parked and grabbed his camera. Ready for action.

Stepping from the car, he was all but swept away by the wind. Strong gusts blew the sand along like the waves in the ocean, creating subtle changes in the landscape. He trudged along, looking around. Always looking. He snapped a couple shots of the incoming waves and some of the dune grass.

Then he saw some tracks. He liked the way they zigzagged along, as if maybe the bird who'd left them was drunk. The bird wasn't in sight, but the tracks had left a record. The blowing sand was fast filling in the indentations, though, and soon all record of the creature having been there would be erased.

Cody focused his camera and snapped several pictures until the tracks were all but gone.

Then he looked back at his own footprints and saw that they, too, were fast fading. He took some shots of them. Now, there was a record of his having been there.

He recalled an old poem a high school English teacher had made the class read, something about footprints in the sands of time. He'd thought it was corny, but now the words took on new meaning.

He couldn't remember the rest of the poem, though. He'd have to ask Luci. She'd remember. She was big on poetry.

He wished she was with him now, to share his trip down the coast. Yeah, like that would work. She'd be good for a few hours, maybe, but then she'd want to head home, to the safety of…of what? Her family? He pushed away thoughts of Luci.

And yet, when he was back in his car and

heading down the highway to the next spur-of-the-moment spot, he couldn't help thinking about her.

Wondering what she was doing.

He slapped his palm against the steering wheel. *Ah, man, no. You don't want to do that. You have places to go. Places you need to see, to experience, to record.*

And that was the way it should be.

"I WAS DISAPPOINTED when Cody and I ran out of photo paper at the contest Saturday," Luci said.

Tessa put down the handful of brochures she was sorting and shot Luci a defiant look. "I took the exact number you had on your list."

Luci laid the list on the table and pointed to the item in question. "The number of packs is right here—eight. We only had five."

Tessa squinted at the number. "That looks like a five to me."

"Then when I came back to get more paper, I couldn't find the key to the supply room in my desk."

"I know I put it back."

"You did, but in the wrong drawer. I found it this morning."

"So I screwed up." Tessa folded her arms. "I stayed in the tent all day, even though it was boring and Carl was out having a good time."

"You did stay, and I appreciate that, but—"

Glen stuck his head in the door. "We need to talk about the contest, Luci. My office."

"Uh-oh." Tessa rolled her eyes.

Luci followed Glen into his office. His mouth was pulled into a tight line, but then, he often looked grim. When they were seated, the shiny desk between them, Glen opened a file folder. They discussed the budget, which she'd kept well within, the number of entrants, which had increased from the previous year, and the number of businesses who set up tents, which had also increased.

"Lots of pluses," Glen said. "Unfortunately, a few minuses keep me from giving you an A on your report card. There were complaints from people who couldn't claim the photos because you ran out of paper."

"That's true, and when I returned to the office to get more, I was delayed because I couldn't find the key to the supply room."

"Better planning would have prevented running out of paper, wouldn't it?"

"Everyone eventually got their photos, and we gave extra coupons to those who had to wait."

He raised his eyebrows. "I wonder how the businesses involved will like that when they agreed on one coupon to a customer."

Luci bit back a retort. Explaining didn't do any good, because he always had to have the last word. She let a few seconds elapse and then said, "Was there anything else? I need to work on the article for *Coastal Living*. The one you wanted me to write about Pine Lake."

"I hope you're making the resort look good."

She nodded and left the room. When she huffed back into her office, Tessa took one look at her and said, "You look mad."

"I'm not mad."

Tessa planted her hands on her hips. "You told him about me messing up, didn't you? I knew you would."

"No, Tessa, I didn't mention your name once."

Tessa widened her eyes. "Why not? I screwed up, didn't I?"

"Yes, you did. But you know what I think? I think you screw up on purpose."

"That's silly. Why would I?"

"For one thing, you're living up to what your father says about you. 'Dad says I'm a screwup and dad knows best, so I must be.' But, more importantly, you make mistakes because you're hoping if I complain to Glen, he'll let you go. And then you can hang out with Carl all day."

Tessa's face turned red, and she didn't say anything for several long seconds. Then she lifted her chin and said, "I could do something really bad, you know."

"I know, but you won't."

"Why?"

"Because you're a better person than you think you are, Tessa. And deep down, you want to do what's right."

"HEY, LUCI."

Luci looked up from collecting papers the printer spit out to see Cody saunter into the office. His jaw was clean shaven and his short-sleeved shirt and jeans looked freshly pressed. Why, oh why, she thought for the hundredth time, did he have to be so handsome?

"Cody. How was your getaway?"

"Great." He rested his hands on his hips. "Maybe you'll come with me sometime—for a day trip," he added hastily.

She tapped the papers on the desk and stapled them together. "We've done day trips—to Cranberry Acres, Pine Lake…"

"Yeah, but for those, we had a mission. I'm talking about going off with nowhere in mind, no agenda. Going where the spirit moves us to go."

"What would that accomplish?"

"You never know. I got some spectacular shots this last trip."

"I'd like to see them. Maybe there are some we can use."

"You've already got 'em. Check your email."

Luci went to her computer and brought up her inbox. Sure enough, there were Cody's pictures. "Pull up a chair," she said, "and I'll take a look."

Cody retrieved a chair and sat beside Luci while she opened the file. The first picture, of billowy clouds lit from behind, burst onto the screen with a brilliance that took her breath away. "Wow. That is spectacular."

"I had to wait hours for that shot," he said, grinning. "I saw a picture developing as the clouds came in and the sun lowered. And then, suddenly, bam, there it was."

Luci brought a new photo to the screen. "What's this?"

"Bird prints in the sand. Look at the next picture and see nature's disappearing act."

Luci clicked on the next photo. "I see. The tracks are fading as the blowing sand fills them in."

"Right. This made me think about a poem from high school English class, something about 'the sands of time.' Ms. Snodgrass was the teacher. You must have had her, too."

Luci gazed at the ceiling and then snapped her fingers. "The poem is 'A Psalm of Life,' by Henry Wadsworth Longfellow, and the part you're thinking of goes like this.

"'Lives of great men all remind us
We can make our lives sublime,
And, departing, leave behind us
Footprints on the sands of time.'"

He sat back and stared. "Now, I'm impressed. Anyway, I thought the poem went with the photos."

"It does." Luci studied the photo again, her mind working. "Have you ever thought of doing a photo essay?"

"It crossed my mind, but I never could settle down long enough to write the words. Or even think of them," he added with a laugh. "I need a writer to do that." He let a few seconds go by and then said, "Do you, ah, know anyone who might be interested?"

"No," she said, sensing where his inquiry was leading and not wanting to go there. "I really don't...know of anyone."

Later, after Cody left, Luci wondered why he'd want to collaborate with her. Working together at the chamber was enough of a challenge. She would stick to her job and let him stick to his. They'd both be better off that way.

CHAPTER SEVENTEEN

LUCI STUDIED HER reflection in the full-length mirror on her closet door. The last time she'd worn a dress was to a graduation party at the U, but Sylvie and Ben's wedding called for something more festive than the slacks and tops she wore to work. And so, she'd chosen a dress made of a lightweight fabric in a shade of bright blue that complemented her red hair. The flared skirt fell to just below her knees, and the top had a flattering scoop neckline. Since the ceremony was on the beach, she wore flats rather than high heels.

Satisfied with her appearance, she grabbed a jacket and her purse and went out the patio door.

Sylvie and Ben would exchange their vows by the Beach Café, where the reception would take place. By the time Luci reached the spot, many other attendees had arrived and the rows of folding chairs were filling up. She spotted Eva and Mark Townson. Sitting with them were their son, Elijah, and daughter, Sasha. Eva spotted her and waved. "Come join us."

Luci sat beside Eva and exchanged greetings with Mark and the children. Then she said, "I can't wait to see what Sylvie is wearing."

"You can bet it won't be the traditional white," Eva said with a chuckle.

A quartet that included the guitar players from Toby's Bar and Grill provided music. Cody was on the job as official photographer, taking candid shots of the guests as they arrived. Spotting Luci and the Townsons, he came over and snapped a few shots of them.

Ben and his best man came to stand at the front. He was older and resembled Ben enough to be his brother, Luci thought. Pastor Jackson from the Community Church joined them, book in hand. Ben's white shirt had a shiny look, as if it might be silk, and his jacket had a carnation in the lapel.

Sylvie's matron of honor was her longtime employee at the souvenir shop. Her two children kept running up to her, and she had to keep shooing them back to their seats with their father.

Finally, Pastor Jackson raised his arms and said, "Let us begin."

Everyone stood and turned to watch Sylvie come down the aisle. Hal Barnett, the man Sylvie always said was like a father to her, gave her away.

Her dress was made of layers and layers of lace, in all colors of the rainbow. The skirt rose and fell with the breeze and swirled about her legs, as though she were floating rather than walking. Her hair was upswept, as usual, but with more tendrils framing her face, and she wore a small hat made of feathers the same colors as those in her dress. Luci would bet Sylvie was the most exotic bird Ben had ever seen.

When the vows had been said—Sylvie's rambled, while Ben's were short and to the point—they turned to face their guests as husband and wife. Everyone clapped and cheered.

The newlyweds walked down the aisle, Sylvie smiling and waving, Ben with his chest thrust out and his head high. At the end of the aisle, all the young women gathered for the toss of Sylvie's bouquet. Sylvie threw the flowers high into the air. A noisy scramble followed, and then one woman held up the bouquet. She ran off to join a young man who looked more scared than happy.

As the sun set and twilight settled over the beach, the wedding party trooped into the Beach Café's banquet room. Round tables, each covered with a brightly colored cloth, filled the room. A dish of flowers sat in the center of each table, and wooden birds from Sylvie's shop held place cards in their beaks.

Luci sat with an out-of-town couple she didn't know. Cody was supposed to be on her other side, but he wasn't there; he was busy taking pictures. By the time he visited the buffet table and sat down with his dinner, everyone else had finished eating. Still, Luci wished Sylvie, or whoever had made the seating assignments, hadn't placed her and Cody together.

He stayed long enough to eat and exchange a few words with Luci and the others at the table, and then he was gone again. "My, he's busy, isn't he?" commented a woman sitting across from Luci.

"I've heard he's a very good photographer," another woman said.

"He is," Luci confirmed.

After dinner, the men made toasts. When Ben gave his, he thanked everyone for coming and then added, "And thanks to the couple that brought Sylvie and me together, Luci Monroe and our esteemed photographer, Cody Jarvis. Stand up, Luci. And Cody's somewhere around here. Oh, there he is, taking my picture." Ben beamed into Cody's camera.

Luci stood and waved. Cody waved, too, and then caught Luci's eye and grinned. She smiled back, but her lips were stiff. Ben had made it sound as though Cody and Luci had planned to get him and Sylvie together.

He'd also called Cody and Luci a couple and, of course, that wasn't true. But then, *couple* didn't have to mean a romantic couple. She shouldn't be so sensitive.

The musicians took up their instruments and began playing a waltz. Sylvie and Hal danced, and then he handed her over to Ben. Ben and Sylvie danced while gazing into each other's eyes, which elicited sighs from the women at Luci's table. After that, other couples filled the floor. A man who worked in her office building, whom she spoke to occasionally in the hallway, asked Luci to dance. Then a friend of Ben's from Seattle approached, and she danced a few songs with him. She'd just sat down when Cody appeared.

"My turn," he said.

"You're finished taking pictures?"

He laughed. "The day I finish taking pictures will be the day I die. But am I finished here at the wedding? No, but I can take a break. I stashed my gear at the front desk."

"Just so you could dance?"

"Just so I could dance with *you*." He held out his arms. "So let's get with it."

"So romantic," she said, then wished she hadn't.

Still, as his arms went around her, she couldn't help the soft sigh that escaped her lips. Being close to him felt wonderful. She liked the way he held her hand against his chest. He was a smooth dancer, too, and they moved in perfect time to the music.

Cody whispered in her ear, his warm breath sending tingles down her spine. The only words she caught were "a couple."

"Yes, that's what Ben called us," she said.

"No, I meant Ben and Sylvie. They make a good couple."

Heat crept up her neck. Of course, he wasn't talking about the two of them. The word *couple* was giving her fits today. "Oh, right. They do…make a good couple."

When the song was over, she expected him to let her go, but he kept his arm around her. "How about another one?"

She opened her mouth to say she'd better be going home, but the words wouldn't come. "All right," she said instead. This might be the only chance she had to be in his arms before he left town.

Ben and Sylvie danced up to them. "Did you get pictures of my aunt Jessie?" Ben managed to say before they swept by.

"Will do," Cody said.

When the song was over, Luci drew away. He pulled her close again. "One more."

She put her hands on his chest. "What about Aunt Jessie?"

"Okay…you're right. I'm on the job. But I'll walk you back to our table."

As they passed the buffet, Cody nodded toward a woman wearing an ankle-length dress. She was piling cookies onto a paper plate.

"There's Aunt Jessie," he said. "That's where she was when we first started dancing."

"She looks happy."

"She *is* a happy person. Her smile lights up the camera."

Before they reached their table, Luci stopped. "I'm not sitting down again. I'm going home now."

His eyes reflected disappointment. "Aw, I wish you'd wait till I'm through."

"Why? You're not worried about me walking home alone, are you? Like after the sand-castle contest?"

He frowned. "I don't like the idea of you being out alone late at night. Not even in Willow Beach."

"So protective," she said, heading toward the door.

He kept up with her. "I try to be a gentleman."

"I do appreciate that, but who's going to watch over me when you leave town?"

His expression sobered. "That's a good question, Luci. I'll have to think on that."

She held up a hand. "No more matchmaking, though. One wedding this summer is enough."

"Even if the next one would be yours?" He was grinning again.

"Even if," she said and before he could say any more, she turned and walked out the door.

CHAPTER EIGHTEEN

"HAVE YOU THOUGHT any more about taking a day trip with me?" Cody asked.

Luci sat back in her desk chair and laced her fingers together. "Not really. But I still don't understand why it's so important. Why do you need my company?"

"Do I have to have a reason?" he teased.

"Maybe you don't, but I do."

"Okay, all the trips we've made together have been planned practically down to the minute."

"That's how I operate. You know that."

"I know, and I'm not saying there's anything wrong with organization. But I'd like to show you my way, just once. You won't have to worry about a thing. No lists. No agenda. Nothing to do but relax. Let what happens happen." Catching her puzzled expression, he added, "For taking pictures."

"Of course. For pictures."

"Come on, Luci, let the plan be no plan. Summer's almost over and I'll—"

She looked away. "Be leaving soon. I know. Do you have your next assignment, by the way?"

"Not yet, but I have a lot of queries out. I'm not worried." Cody cleared his throat and avoided Luci's gaze. Actually, he was concerned. Time was running out and summer was almost over. He needed to be planning his next trip.

"Glen might not like me running off on something as vague as this outing appears to be."

"Then we'll go on a Saturday."

Luci sighed. "You're making it very hard for me to say no."

"Good. Saturday it is. I'll pick you up at nine."

Cody left the office shaking his head. What was he thinking? Why did he want to keep pushing his lifestyle on her? What was he trying to prove?

He kept arguing with himself, on and off, right up until Saturday when he loaded the car and went to pick her up. He even stopped at the entrance to her cul-de-sac, wondering whether he should text her that something had come up and the trip was off. But then he looked down the street and saw her waiting for him.

She stood on the steps outside her front door, a backpack at her feet. Her red hair shone in the rays of the sun, which was rising over the housetops. Man, she was beautiful. Awed by the sight, he pulled out his camera, focused his telephoto lens and brought her in close. Yes, that pert nose, those perfect lips... He snapped several shots before he finally put down the camera.

Cody stopped in front of her apartment and jumped out of his SUV. Fighting the urge to pull her into his arms and kiss her, he stepped back and let his gaze travel over her instead. Blue T-shirt and hoodie, jeans and athletic shoes. Perfect.

"Lookin' good, Luci."

"Glad I pass inspection."

She reached to pick up her backpack, but he grabbed it first. He loaded it into the back of the car and then helped her to climb in.

"Such a gentleman," she teased.

"Such a lady," he teased back. Today was going to be a good day.

"So where are we going?" she asked as they started winding their way over to Main Street.

"Aha. Lesson number one. I don't know where we're going. But we've got everything we need." He took his hand from the wheel and indicated the space behind them. "All my gear, of course, and that cooler back there? Plenty of food. I stopped at Max's grocery store on the way over and picked up some sandwiches from their deli."

"I thought this was a no-plan day."

He held up two fingers. "Lesson number two. Food is an exception. I do plan for that. Don't want to get caught out in the wilds somewhere on an empty stomach."

"Good to know."

They traveled down Main, stopping for a couple of traffic lights. When they reached the Thank You for Visiting Willow Beach sign, the road split off. Straight ahead would take them down the coast. A left turn led inland.

"Which way should we go?" he asked.

She shrugged. "I don't know. This is your show."

"Yeah, but you're allowed input. In fact, I want your input."

"I'm at a loss on this one."

Cody pulled onto the wide shoulder. He leaned back, dug into his jeans pocket and pulled out a coin. "We'll let this decide." He held up a quarter. "Your call."

"Okay, heads we continue down the coast, tails we go inland."

Cody flipped the coin, caught it and turned it over on the back of his hand. He showed it to her.

"Tails," she said.

"And so, as they say, the die is cast."

"Are we going to let the coin decide everything?" she asked after he'd turned onto the road they'd chosen.

"Nope. I've also got a crystal ball, a pack of tarot cards and a pair of dice we can use," he replied, careful to keep a straight face.

She nodded with mock solemnity. "That's reassuring."

They drove on. He turned on the radio and found his favorite country-western station. After several songs, the DJ played "Travelin' Man."

"Hey, there's my song," Cody said. "That's what I am, a travelin' man."

"You are," she said. "And you're happy that way."

"Yes, I am."

The affirmation didn't come out as convincingly as usual. He glanced at her. Had she heard the doubt in his voice? He couldn't tell because she was turned away, gazing out the passenger window.

After a few miles, he began looking for a turnoff. "Lesson three," he said, "find some action." He spotted a road. "That looks promising."

She peered out the windshield. "I'm curious to know exactly what makes it promising. It looks like an ordinary road to me."

"It's promising because I don't know where it leads. I can't see the end of it and there's no sign that tells me. I'll have to drive down it to know what I'll find."

"Maybe you'll find a sign that says Private. No Trespassing."

He shrugged. "Maybe."

After they'd gone about a mile, the road narrowed, and another mile after that the pavement ended. They bumped in and out of potholes. But it was still a road, although meeting a vehicle coming in the opposite direction might prove difficult. He slowed, while they both looked around.

"There's another road leading off that way."

"Good eye," he said and swung onto it.

This road was even narrower than the one they'd been on, with bushes and tree branches swiping the sides and even the roof of the car.

"I see water up ahead," he said after a while.

"I do, too. It looks like a stream."

The road finally ended near the water's edge. "There are other tire marks here," he said.

"Somebody's fishing spot?"

"That'd be my guess. A spot they don't want anyone to know about."

"Don't tell me you brought your fishing pole."

He laughed. "No, I didn't, but that's a good idea."

They got out. He rummaged in the back and retrieved his camera, all set up with the telephoto lens. Then he pulled out another, smaller camera and handed it to Luci.

"What's this?"

"You gotta do the whole thing." He looped the strap around her neck.

"But I'm not a photographer."

"You are today. This camera's a simple aim and shoot. It'll do everything on its own."

"Even while I'm napping?" she teased.

"No napping allowed. Come on, let's see what the stream has to offer."

They walked to the edge and stood watching the silver-gray water flow over rocks and a few fallen branches until it disappeared around a bend. On the other side was a wood with tall, skinny pine trees and bushes that sprouted red berries. The wood wasn't thick enough to blot out the sun entirely, and here and there its rays gave everything a golden glow.

He snapped a couple of shots and then noticed that Luci was taking pictures, too. He didn't ask of what. Let her do her thing.

A splash broke the silence. He lowered his camera. "What was that?"

"A fish jumped," she said. "I saw it. Right over there where those rocks are sticking up."

"All ri-ight." He hunkered down at the edge of the water. Camera poised, waiting.

Another fish broke the surface, but he missed it. "I'm slow on the draw today," he said. He glanced at her, saw her camera up to her eye.

The fish jumped again. "You get it?" he asked.

She shook her head. "I'm too slow."

"Keep trying."

Finally, three or four jumps later, he landed the shot. Cody showed her the picture. "Look at the curve of that baby. Look how the light shines on the drops of water rolling off him."

"Uh-huh. Like a gold necklace."

He tilted his head and studied her. "That's nice."

"What?"

"What you just said. Write it down."

"What? I didn't bring any paper with me."

"Record it on your phone."

"Well...okay." She pulled out her phone and spoke the words and then shook her head. "You're crazy."

He laughed. "I hope you had the speaker turned off when you said that."

He took some more pictures, and so did she. Noticing the sun was almost overhead, he said, "We'd better move on. Who knows what we're missing somewhere else."

They continued down the highway, turning off here and there as the spirit moved them. They ate lunch sitting under a tree on a hillside and after that meandered through a forest where a doe led her two fawns along a shady path. In one spot, jackrabbits hopped in a field, and in another butterflies hovered over wildflowers growing against a wooden fence.

As he often did, Cody lost track of time. Then he noticed the shadows were long and skinny instead of short and fat. "Time for a break," he said as he pulled into the next roadside rest stop.

"I can't believe the whole day has passed," Luci said a few minutes later. They sat at a picnic bench sipping coffee provided by the stop's volunteers.

"We're not done yet. There's a full moon tonight. Can't miss that."

"I don't think I can last that long."

"Aw, come on, you're getting into this. You've taken some great pictures and recorded some great descriptions."

She tilted her head and narrowed her eyes. "Is that what this is all about? You getting my free writing service?"

"No. This is about..." *About us spending*

time together. "About me giving you a taste of what I like to do," he said.

"Why?"

Because when you love someone, you want to share your life with that person.

Cody blinked and shook his head. Luci raised her eyebrows, waiting for his answer.

"Because we're friends." Oh, man, that sounded lame.

He drank some more coffee and then cast her another covert glance. She was looking off into the trees, her expression sad. He jumped up and held out his hand. "C'mon, let's get going, before we're out of sunlight."

At dinnertime, they stopped at a restaurant for clam chowder and fish and chips. "How're you holding up?" he asked.

Luci finished munching a French fry. "I feel like I've put in a full day's work."

"You have. A lot different from sitting behind a desk, though, huh?"

She offered a rueful smile. "There were times today when my desk chair would have felt pretty comfortable."

Cody speared a bite of his fish. "Yeah, this lifestyle can come with a price. But the rewards make up for any hardship."

"For you, maybe."

He looked up. "But not for you? You can't see yourself doing what we did today?"

"No. It takes more than just pointing and shooting to do what you do. You have an eye for it. A talent. I'm skilled with words."

"Pictures need words."

"Not always. Remember that old saying, a picture is worth a thousand words? You don't need my words, Cody. Your photos speak for themselves."

But I need you.

Man, that voice in his head was sure busy today.

When they finished their meals, he tried again. "Sure I can't talk you into making a night of it? I've got a couple sleeping bags."

She shook her head. "I need to get back."

"Got a date?" he teased and then held his breath waiting for her answer.

She smiled. "Just with my computer."

"Never had to compete with a computer before," he said.

"Anyone who tries to date you will have to compete with a camera."

"Ouch," he said and reached for the check.

THEY DIDN'T TALK much on the way home. Cody was tired, too, so maybe cutting the trip short was a good thing.

When they reached her apartment, she turned to him, her eyes apologetic in the fading light. "You won't get your feelings hurt if I don't invite you in?"

"No. I'm pretty beat, too. Walk you to the door, though."

"It was fun, getting a peek into your life," she said when they reached her doorstep.

"Glad you could come with me today."

They stood there, the hum of the surf and the cool night air swirling around them. Should he kiss her or not? He always gave her a peck on the cheek. Except for the night of the sand-castle contest. That kiss had been a real kiss, her lips sweet and warm, his arms wound tight around her. Did he want to go there again? Hell, yes. He leaned forward, closed his eyes and aimed for her lips.

And met the softness of her cheek.

Okay, so that's the way it was.

After he left Luci's, he thought about heading out somewhere, anywhere, and catching the moon when it rose. He finally decided to call it a night, too, and drove to his place. The lights in his mother's house were on, and Mel's car stood in the driveway.

Cody parked in front of his apartment and went in. Reviewing his photos usually allowed him to relive the initial excitement of taking the pictures, but tonight, he looked at a few of them and then lost interest. He wandered around, feeling cramped in the small space.

After he made himself a cup of coffee, Cody went outside and sat in a lawn chair. The lights were still on in the main house and the flicker of the TV reflected in the living room window. He could guess the reason. Olive was making Mel watch *Dancing With the Stars*. And Mel, being the congenial guy he was, and also being more than a little crazy about Olive, was sitting there happily munching popcorn and sipping a beer.

Maybe that worked for them, but it wouldn't work for him. And just what had he been trying to prove today by dragging Luci all over the countryside? She said she got it, but did she really? Did he want her to?

He leaned back in his chair and gazed at the sky. Stars were popping out, one by one.

He remembered watching the stars come out when he'd been in Africa, on the plains. The vastness of the land, stretching out as far as the eye could see, kind of reminded him of home. But here the ocean filled the landscape.

It was a big, wide world, and one he hadn't even begun to explore. So much out there waiting for him. Why would he even consider staying here? There was nothing for him. Olive had Mel to take care of her, and Luci, well, Luci had her whole family. She didn't need him. And, someday, the right man for her would come along. He knew one thing: he was not that man.

"WHAT DO YOU MEAN, we're not having family Sunday?" Luci pressed her cell phone to her ear to be sure she heard her father's response. She'd been home from her outing with Cody for only a few minutes before her father called to deliver the shocking announcement.

"We decided to skip it this week."

"*We*? Who's *we*? I don't remember being asked my opinion."

"Your mother and I decided."

"Why? What's wrong?"

"She's not feeling well, and I have work to do." He sounded tired, not at all like his usual energetic self and not all that convincing, either.

"What's wrong with Mom? And why are you suddenly working at home so much? You never used to do that." Luci paced to her patio door and gazed out at the rapidly darkening sky.

"So many questions, Luci. Your mother has a headache. Something she ate, she thinks. And I have a lot of extra work, that's all. We're very busy at the bank."

"What about Don and Arliss, and Francine and Will?"

"Don's going fishing, and Arliss is taking the kids to a birthday party. Francine's showing houses, as usual, and Will said he didn't want Anna to cook if she wasn't feeing well."

"I'd be glad to do the cooking."

"No, no," he said quickly. "We've already decided."

"I'm sorry Mom's not feeling well, but I'm also disappointed. One of the main reasons I came back to Willow Beach was because of our family. We've always been so close..."

She wanted him to reassure her that the family was still close. But he remained silent. She sensed he was waiting for her to say goodbye and hang up.

Which she did.

As she bent to switch on the lamp by the sofa, she saw the yellow bowl and the photo album. Luci dropped onto the sofa and picked up the bowl. She ran her fingers over the smooth surface, recalling all the times she'd seen it displaying her mother's roses at the family home.

She put down the bowl and picked up the album. She paged through the pictures, stopping to look at those of her family. Everyone looked happy.

So much had changed since then, and looking at the photos now brought a painful tightness to her chest. Tears blurring her eyes, she closed the album.

What had happened to her dream?

THE FOLLOWING MORNING, Luci finished eating her oatmeal and toast and washed her dishes. She stood in the center of her apartment, looking around. Now what? With no family Sunday, she had the whole day with nothing to do. Okay, she could do housework. She got out the vacuum cleaner and swept and dusted. Opening the patio door, her gaze fell on the flowers her mother had planted. She hoped Anna was recovering from her headache. She'd call home later and see how she was feeling.

As the day wore on, finding something to do posed a challenge. She thought about calling one of her friends, but the ones here in town were all married with their own families and their own Sunday plans. The singles had moved away. Maybe she should move away, too. Maybe she didn't belong here anymore.

But where would she go?

As she wandered aimlessly around the apartment, her thoughts turned to Cody and yesterday's outing. What had that been about? He'd wanted her to share his enthusiasm for his life's work. Well, fine. But why, when he'd be leaving soon.

Or had yesterday been his roundabout way

of asking her to share his life? Was she being tested to see if he wanted to take their relationship to the next level? Whatever that was.

Her gaze fell on her computer. She sat at the table and turned it on.

Cody had sent her some of the photos they'd taken yesterday. "For your files," his message read.

Viewing the photos would only remind her of their time together, and she wasn't sure she wanted to think about that any more. But, with nothing else to do, she might as well take a look.

The pictures of the fish jumping brought a smile to her lips. He'd liked what she'd said about that, something about "a golden necklace." She hunted up the notes on her phone and read them. Hmm, maybe she could take that idea a bit further. Why not? She had nothing else to do.

She put the best of the fish photos in a separate box, with her words underneath. Then she added some more text as the words came to her, revisiting the moment when the fish leaped from the water, arcing into the air as though saying, "Look at me. Look what I can do."

She sat back and read what she'd written. Not bad. She brought up the next picture, one of the stream and the opposite bank. The sun carved a path through the pine trees. A path leading where? She thought about that for a while and when an idea came to her, she wrote it under the photo. She'd worked her way through half-a-dozen photos by the time she realized she was doing exactly what Cody had wanted her to do: adding text to his pictures.

After a while, she turned to the pictures she had taken and was soon adding text to those.

Kinda fun, really.

But probably a waste of time.

Still, she had gained a better understanding of Cody's love of spontaneity.

She shut down the computer and ended the day with a walk on the beach. At least she had the beach. She'd loved walking along the shore since she was a toddler holding on to her mother's hand.

The beach was like an old friend. She loved listening to the soft shushing of the waves, the calls of the gulls and the singing of the wind in the dune grass. Placing her feet in the sand, one step after another, while gazing out to sea…to forever, soothed her troubled spirit. And today it didn't let her down.

CHAPTER NINETEEN

HER MOTHER'S GARDEN, always so neat and well tended, was dry and full of weeds. Anna must be really sick, Luci thought. Her chest tight with worry, she grabbed the vase of flowers and hurried into the house.

"Hello!" No one answered her greeting. Her mother was nowhere to be seen. Usually, if not in her garden, she could be found in the kitchen or in her sewing room stitching quilts for the church's Christmas bazaar.

Luci climbed the stairs and went down the hall to her parents' bedroom. The door was open. The bed had the covers tossed back on one side, with the other side undisturbed. The bathroom door stood open. She crossed the room and peeked in. No one was there, but the scent of her father's aftershave lingered in the air.

She continued down the hall. The doors to all the bedrooms were open except the one to

Francine's former room. Luci knocked on the door. "Mom, are you in there? It's me, Luci."

"I'm not feeling well, Luci," came her mother's muffled voice.

"I know, but can I come in?"

"If you must."

Juggling the vase in one hand, Luci opened the door. The blinds were closed, and the room was dim and stuffy. Her mother lay in bed, her face turned toward the wall.

Luci approached the bed. "I brought you something."

Her mother slowly turned her head. Her eyes were red rimmed.

"From the Blossom Shop." Luci set the bouquet on the nightstand.

"They're beautiful, dear. Thank you."

Luci sat on the end of the bed. "Mom, what's wrong? Dad said you've been having headaches. Have you seen a doctor?"

"No. I'll be all right. I'll get up later."

"Is there anything I can do?"

"No, dear. Don't you have to be at work today?"

Luci smoothed a wrinkle in the bedspread. "I do. I just wanted to check on you during my lunch hour."

"Could you hand me a tissue, please?"

"Sure." Luci picked up the box of tissues from the nightstand and held it out.

Anna sat up and plucked out a tissue. She wiped her eyes and then lay back down. "You'd better go now. I don't want you to get into trouble with Glen."

"All right, but call me if you need anything. Promise?"

"I promise." Anna sighed and closed her eyes.

Checking her watch, Luci saw the time was now one thirty. Still, before she left, she tidied up the kitchen and watered the garden.

Her mother's roses reminded her of the time when she was learning to ride her two-wheeled bike. She'd fallen off and skinned her knee and collapsed into tears. Her mother had bandaged her wound and then brought her a rose. "Smell this," she'd said, "and you'll feel better."

Luci had inhaled the sweet scent and as her mother promised, she felt better. Perhaps that was why she'd brought flowers today—hoping a bouquet would comfort her mother. Sadly, that hadn't been the case.

When Luci entered the chamber office,

Marge looked up from her desk. "Glen's looking for you."

"Oh? Something important?"

Marge gave a cynical-sounding laugh. "With him, everything's important. Pressure, pressure."

Luci hadn't gone far down the hall when Glen stepped from one of the offices. "Luci, there you are. You get held up at lunch?" He tapped his wristwatch. "It's past one."

"I know. I stopped by my parents' house to check on my mother. She's not feeling well."

He fell into step beside her as she continued on to her office. "Sorry to hear that, but shouldn't your father be the one to take care of her?"

"Our family is close, Glen. We all take care of each other."

"Hmm, well, that's nice, but we have a business to run here."

"I know and I'm back now. Was there something in particular you wanted to see me about?" They reached her open office door and she turned to face him.

"Yes. The printer's waiting for the copy for the new brochures."

Luci closed her eyes. "That's right. It was due—"

"Last Friday."

"I'll take care of it right away."

"See that you do." He swiveled around and headed back down the hall.

As Luci entered her office, Tessa turned from her station at the worktable. "I thought maybe you were taking the rest of the day off," she said.

"I had some personal business to take care of."

"Uncle Glen's been in and out for the past hour."

"I saw him on my way in. Everything's under control."

Actually, everything was not under control. Luci still hadn't finished writing the copy for several of the brochures. She'd completely forgotten about the printer's deadline because she'd been preoccupied by the family's troubles. She had no one to blame but herself for this predicament.

Luci looked up the printer's number and called him.

"We're on a tight schedule," Joe Manning

said when he came on the line. "I needed your stuff on Friday."

"What if I got it to you first thing tomorrow?"

"Hold on, lemme check."

Luci waited. In the background, machinery whirred, a door slammed, someone shouted and someone else laughed.

Joe finally returned. "You get it here eight a.m., I can make it work. Maybe."

"Thanks, Joe. I owe you one."

"S'okay, I owe your dad a few. He gave me a good deal on a loan, few years back."

Luci shook her head as she hung up. Was there anyone in town who didn't owe her father a favor?

Now, to finish the brochures. She opened the file and started to work. Thankfully, most of the updates in this batch had already been done.

She'd been working for a few minutes, concentrating hard, when she became aware of Tessa standing behind her. "Did you want something, Tessa?" she asked over her shoulder.

"Can I help?"

The sincerity in Tessa's voice took Luci

by surprise. She whirled around and stared. "You want to help?"

Tessa frowned. "Okay, so you don't want me to." She took a step away.

Luci held up her hand. "No, no, wait. I, ah, yes, you can help." She searched her mind. "How about proofreading? Finding any mistakes I might have made."

"I know what proofreading is, and doesn't your computer do that?"

Luci winced at the return of Tessa's defensive tone. Still, this was the first time she had asked if she could help instead of waiting to be told what to do. Maybe they were making progress.

"The word processing program doesn't always catch everything," Luci said. "It takes a human eye, too. So, if you'll do that, I have the copy on the lighthouse ready to print out."

"Okay."

Luci hit a couple keys and in a few seconds the printer hummed. Tessa plucked the paper from the tray and took it to her seat. For the next few minutes, they both worked in silence, the only sounds the ringing of Marge's phone and Glen, having a conversation in the hallway.

When Tessa finished reading the copy, she approached Luci's desk. Luci stopped typing. "What'd you find?"

Tessa held out the paper and pointed to a spot. "Shouldn't this be a capital *L* because it's part of the official name of the lighthouse?"

Luci inspected the copy. "Yes, it should. Good eye, Tessa."

Tessa stood taller and smiled. "I could do another. It's easy and the photos are cool. Like this one." She indicated the photo on the brochure's cover, showing the lighthouse and the rock promontory it sat on, as well as a glimpse of the beach below.

"Yes, Cody is a good photographer."

"He's nice, too. He said he'd help me with taking pictures, if I wanted."

"Oh, when did he say that?"

"At the sand-castle contest. When we were setting up. Only there wasn't time that day. And soon I'll be leaving."

Her voice held a wistful note and once again, Luci registered surprise. "Won't you be glad to go back home?"

"Oh, I don't know. This place kinda grows on you."

Luci laughed. "I know what you mean."

The afternoon passed, and both Luci and Tessa made progress. For the first time, Luci felt as though they were a team. Then, a knocking on the window captured her attention.

Carl. She might've guessed.

He peered in, one hand at his brow to block out the sunlight, the other poised to knock on the glass again. Luci sighed. Tessa squealed and tossed down the brochure she was proofing. She ran to the window. He spread his palm on the glass, and she matched his with hers.

"Tessa…" Luci began.

"Okay if I go a little early today?" Tessa pleaded.

"How early?"

"Like now?"

Luci checked her wristwatch. Four-thirty. Still half an hour until quitting time. Carl had turned from the window, stuck his hands in the back pockets of his cargo pants and paced to the fountain and back, glancing at them every now and then.

"You leave early lots of times," Tessa said.

"Yes, when I have somewhere to go on business."

"You said you were late today because of personal business."

Luci couldn't argue with that. "All right. You have been especially helpful today. Go."

"Thanks. You're the best."

Watching Tessa sprint toward the door brought to mind an adage Luci's mother used to quote—one step forward, two steps back. Yep, that certainly fit her relationship with Tessa. Shaking her head, she turned back to her work.

CHAPTER TWENTY

THE FOLLOWING MORNING, Luci was working at her computer when Cody arrived. "Are you okay?" he asked after they'd exchanged greetings.

Luci yawned. "Tired. Didn't get much sleep last night."

"What was that about?" He lowered his voice and added, "Or shouldn't I ask?"

"No secret. I forgot a deadline for the printer and was up late finishing the brochures."

"You shoulda called me."

"Nothing you could do, Cody."

"Oh, I don't know. Keep the coffee hot. Hold your hand." He grinned. "That's what friends are for, aren't they?"

"Thanks for the offer, but it's done now and delivered this morning. Your photos are great, by the way. Take a look at the printouts on Tessa's table."

He walked over and picked up the new brochures. "Not like you to forget a deadline, Luci," he said as he flipped through the pages.

"Yeah, well, I've had a lot on my mind. That's my excuse, anyway. Not that Glen would buy it."

Cody looked up. "He give you a bad time?"

She waved her hand. "Oh, the usual."

He put down the brochures and went to look out the window. "Are you sorry you went with me on Saturday?" he asked in a low tone.

"No, Cody, not sorry. None of this is your fault."

"Did you get the photos I sent you from our trip?"

"I did."

"Did you, ah, do anything with them? Not that you had to or anything..."

"If you mean, did I write any captions, okay, I might have written a few."

He turned and shot her a smile. "Hey, great. Can I see?"

"I'll email them to you."

"Okay." He looked around. "Where's your assistant, by the way?"

"She went to the post office on an errand for Marge."

"I hope she's back by lunchtime."

Luci shook her head. "I'm not going out to lunch today. I want to get started on the PR for the clambake the chamber puts on in September."

"It's just one party after another around here," he said. Then he sobered and looked out the window again. "I'll have to miss that."

"You're leaving soon?"

"I signed on for the summer, remember? The regular photographer will be returning soon. He'll be your go-to guy for the clambake photos."

Luci's throat tightened. At the beginning of the summer, she hadn't wanted to work with Cody. Now, she couldn't imagine working without him.

"Do you know where you're going?" she asked.

"Not sure. My buddies and I are still working on a few possibilities."

"Your buddies?"

"Yeah, Dex and Shar. I told you about them."

"Oh, right. But you haven't mentioned them for a while, and I forgot about them."

"We've been keeping in touch. In fact, they should be here—" he consulted his wristwatch "—just about now."

Marge appeared in the doorway. "Two people here to see you, Cody." She stood aside and a man and a woman burst into the room. The woman ran straight to Cody and threw her arms around him. "We found you!" she said.

"Hello, Shar." Cody pulled her into an embrace, and they exchanged a kiss on the cheek.

Then Cody let go of Shar and extended a hand to the man. "Hey, Dex."

"Thought we'd never get here." Dex pumped Cody's hand.

One arm around each of their shoulders, Cody said, "Luci, Marge, meet my best buddies ever—Sharlene Williams and Dexter Hunter. Better known as Shar and Dex."

Marge nodded and fluttered her fingers. "Pleased to meet you. Now I'd better get back to my desk." She turned and disappeared down the hall.

Luci stood and approached the newcomers. "Hello. I've heard about you both."

"We've heard about you, too," Shar said, as she and Luci shook hands. A blonde with big brown eyes and full lips, Shar looked cool and casual in jeans and a sleeveless shirt.

Dex had thick black hair and a neatly trimmed beard. "So this is Luci," he said, clasping her extended hand in both of his. "Your pictures don't do you justice."

Luci raised her eyebrows. "My pictures?"

"The ones he carries." Dex motioned toward Cody while still looking at her.

Luci peeked around Dex's broad shoulder and said, "You carry my picture around?"

Cody grinned. "Yours and about a hundred others. My phone has a lot of storage."

Shar pulled away from Cody and gazed around. "Well, look at you, Mr. Cody Jarvis. Pret-ty fancy digs, I'd say." She twirled toward the window. "A view and everything."

Cody rested his hands on his hips. "Aw, this is Luci's office. I just drop in now and then."

"You've been shooting for this outfit all summer?" Dex directed his question to Cody, but he still hadn't stopped looking at Luci.

"Yeah, I have," Cody said. "It hasn't been so bad. Made a few bucks."

"Now, you're ready to roll again." Shar returned to his side.

"Will be in a week, tops. A few things I need to finish up here."

"Can we continue this fascinating discussion over some food?" Dex patted his stomach. "Breakfast was a long time ago."

"How was the B and B?" Cody asked. "They're staying at The Gables," he said to Luci.

"Pret-ty fancy," Shar said. "At least my room is."

"Beats sleeping in the van." Dex grinned.

Shar nodded. "Oh, yeah."

"So, come on," Dex said, "show me some of that seafood you're supposed to be famous for."

"He's from Denver," Cody said.

Dex gave Luci a wink. "Yep, just an old farm boy."

"And Shar is from Omaha," Cody added.

"Not a farm girl, though," Shar said. "We lived in the city, and my dad worked for one of the neighborhood newspapers."

"So that's how you got into the biz," Cody

said. "I never knew that. And here I thought I knew everything about you."

Shar batted her eyelashes. "Oh, honey, there's a lot you don't know."

Dex cleared his throat. "Okay, you two. Enough, already." He held out his arm to Luci. "May I escort you to lunch?"

Luci shook her head. "No, thanks. I have a lot of work to do."

Dex's mouth turned down. "Was it something I said?"

Luci laughed. "No, not at all."

"Dinner tonight, then. And no excuses." He raised his forefinger.

"All right."

"We'll pick you up at seven."

Dex ambled over to join Cody and Shar, who had linked her arm through Cody's. Dex took Shar's other arm, and the three of them walked to the door together.

"Gotta show you my new lens," Dex was saying. "And Shar's shooting with a new setup, too."

"We have a lot to catch up on," Shar said.

Luci's throat tightened. They were like the Three Musketeers, and she couldn't help envying their camaraderie.

She'd barely turned back to her computer when Tessa breezed in. "Who was that with Cody?" she asked.

"Some photographer friends of his are visiting."

"Duh. I saw their cameras. I mean, who was the guy?"

"His name is Dexter."

"He's cute."

"And way too old for you," Luci said in a stern tone.

Tessa glared. "What are you now, my mother?"

Luci gritted her teeth. "I found some more files that need sorting. They're on your table."

"Bor-ring."

Luci sighed. It was going to be a long afternoon.

LUCI CHECKED OVER the clothes in her closet, wondering what to wear to dinner tonight. Even though a nap had refreshed her, she wished she was staying home instead of going out with Cody and his friends. But, since she'd refused lunch, she'd better join them for dinner.

What to wear, though? She finally decided

to dress down and pulled out a pair of jeans and a T-shirt.

When her doorbell rang, she ran to open the door, expecting to see Cody. But Dex stood there. He still wore jeans but had changed his T-shirt for a long-sleeved sports shirt. Rolled-up sleeves revealed his muscular arms and a stand-up collar framed his square-jawed face.

"Your chariot awaits, madam." He made a sweeping gesture toward the driveway.

A glance over his shoulder revealed not Cody's black SUV, as she had expected, but a dark red SUV.

"Where are Cody and Shar?" she asked.

"They're on a film hunt."

"Film? Who uses film anymore?"

"Lots of us pros do. The old ways are still good ways." He led her out to his car. Like Cody's, the back was converted to hold gear in locked boxes fastened to the floor.

"So, tell me about Luci," Dex said as they drove off.

"What do you already know about me? That will save us some time."

"Hmm, I know you were an intern for the

local rag—the *Herald*, right—when Cody worked there."

"That's right. Later, we were at the University of Washington at the same time, but he graduated a couple years ahead of me. We hadn't seen each other for about a year when he showed up this summer."

Dex turned onto Main Street. "Okay, that tells me about you and him, but what about you?"

She shrugged. "Hometown girl. Close family. Like to write, like to walk the beach." She stopped and laughed self-consciously. "That sounds like one of those personals ads."

"Is it? Are you looking to get hooked up with someone?"

"Well, sure. At some point in my life. Isn't everyone?" Before he could answer, she went on, "But, anyway, my life must sound boring, compared to yours."

"Not to worry, Luci," he said softly. "You're far from being boring."

Uncomfortable with his intimate tone, she turned to look out the window. When she realized they were almost at the end of Main Street, she said, "Where are we going?"

"We're meeting Cody and Shar at Toby's

Bar and Grill. Ah, why the frown? Not an okay place?"

"No, it's fine. I just thought Cody would take you two to someplace a little more—"

"More fancy-shmancy? Nah. We're the loud-music-and-beer type."

When they pulled into the parking lot, she spotted Cody's SUV. "Looks like they're here."

Toby's was packed, including the counter, the booths along the walls and the tables in the middle. Waitresses with trays held aloft pushed their way through the crowd, and Toby, a big guy who was both owner and bartender, stood behind the bar mixing drinks.

Luci stood on tiptoe and peered into the bar's dim interior. "How're we ever going to find them in this crowd?"

"There they are, in a booth over in the corner." Dex grabbed Luci's hand and pushed them through the crowd.

Cody and Shar sat on the same side of the booth, a pitcher of beer and glasses on the table. "You're finally here," Cody said. "Good thing, too. If I had to listen to any more stories from this one, I'd croak."

Shar leaned back and punched his shoulder. "Hey, you love my stories. Quit complaining."

Dexter stood aside and let Luci slip into the booth.

"Speaking of stories, don't believe anything this guy tells you," Cody said. "He's full of it."

Dex grabbed the pitcher and poured two glasses of beer. He handed one to Luci. "Here's to new adventures," he said, raising his glass.

"New adventures," Cody and Shar said in unison.

They all clinked their glasses together and then drank.

"Did you find the film you were looking for?" Luci asked.

Shar rolled her eyes. "Finally. You'd think the drugstore, right? But no. And not the gas station, either."

"So where?" Luci asked.

"Max's grocery store," Cody said. "By the checkout stand."

Luci sipped her beer. "You didn't bring extra?"

"Oh, yeah." Shar fingered the paper coaster

under her glass. "It's at the B and B. Didn't want to run all the way back there for it."

Cody sipped his beer and then caught Luci's eye. "Lookin' good, Luci."

"Thanks. You, too, Cody."

As they continued to gaze at each other, the background noise faded away, and she was aware only of Cody. Warmth flooded her and her heartbeat quickened. Then Dex cleared his throat and said, "Hey, is it time to order a pizza yet?" and the spell was broken.

Shar laughed and tugged Cody's arm. "Leave it to Dex to keep us on the food track."

"I could go for a pizza." Cody pulled the menu card from the metal holder.

"Get one with the works," Dex said. "That ought to make everybody happy."

After the waitress took their order and brought another pitcher of beer, the talk turned to their visit to the lighthouse. The pictures they took were, according to Shar, "Pret-ty good."

"*Screen Shot* might be interested," Cody said, and Shar and Dex nodded.

"That's one of the outfits we sell to," Dex told Luci.

"Ah," she said.

"What'd you use for your surf shots?" Cody asked, launching a discussion filled with technical terms that might as well have been in a foreign language. But Luci smiled politely and asked a question now and then. She was glad when the pizza came—eating gave her something to do.

"I'm stuffed," Dex said after a while, sitting back and patting his stomach. "Now I need some exercise. How 'bout a dance, Miss Luci?"

Catching Cody's frown, she smiled and said, "Sure, Dex."

The dance floor was so crowded they could barely move. "Good thing it's a slow tune," Dex said as the band played a blues number. The singer, a woman wearing a long, slinky gown that looked too fancy for the establishment, poured her heart into the lyrics of a love song—not the kind of song for a dance with a near stranger. But Dex was a perfect gentleman, holding her gently and keeping a respectable distance between them.

After a while, his breath warm in her ear, Dex said, "We're probably boring you to death, right? We tend to get carried away, sometimes."

"Ah, no. It's all very interesting."

"You're sweet to say so."

They danced two more numbers, and then the band struck up a fast song. They looked at each other and both shook their heads. "Too dangerous in this crowd," he yelled. "Don't want you getting poked in the eye with some dude's elbow."

When they returned to the table, Cody and Shar were deep in conversation.

"Where are the cameras?" Dex asked as they slipped into the booth.

"Not to worry," Cody said. "I took them out and locked them up. Now we can all dance without worry. So, how about it, Luci?"

"That's a war zone out there," Dex warned.

"We'll wait for a slow one," Cody said.

When a slow tune came up, Cody took Luci's hand and led her to the dance floor. Being in his arms was different from dancing with Dex, maybe because Cody was familiar and Dex was still a stranger. No, it was more than that, and she knew it. They danced without speaking, which allowed her to focus on just being in his arms. It seemed like forever since they'd danced at Sylvie and Ben's wedding.

When the song ended, she expected to return to the table, but he drew her off the dance floor and into a hallway leading to the back door.

"Where are we going?" she asked.

"I want to talk to you for a minute."

As they stepped outside, the cool air washed over her. It was refreshing after the stuffy bar. Darkness had fallen, and the stars peeked out from behind a light cloud cover. Grasping her shoulders, he leaned her back against the building's brick wall. She gazed up at him. His eyes were dark and serious.

"What's this all about?" she asked.

"About you and Dex."

"What on earth are you talking about?"

"Why are you flirting with him?"

Luci's jaw dropped. When she'd recovered, she said, "Am I hearing right? You think I'm flirting with Dex?"

"Not think—know. And he's flirting back. But you'd never leave Willow Beach to be with a freelancer. And he couldn't stay. You'd only be hurt in the end."

Luci pulled away from him and planted her hands on her hips. "You are something else, Cody."

"What do you mean?"

"First, you try to match me up with Ben, and that didn't work. Now, you want me to stay away from Dex. When will you stop trying to run my love life?"

"We're…friends. Don't friends look out for each other?"

"They do. But you'll be leaving in what? A few more days? A week? You going to look out for me then?"

A noisy group burst through the back door. Cody grasped Luci's hand and pulled her out of their way. The others waved and continued on to the parking lot. He waited until their voices faded into the distance and then said, "You're right, I won't be able to look out for you then."

She almost blurted out, *But that won't stop you from going, will it?* Thankfully, she clamped her jaw shut before the words could escape and went back inside.

LATER, AFTER THEY left Toby's, Luci settled back in the seat of Dex's car and exhaled a relieved breath. Soon she'd be home. Right now, there was no place she'd rather be. Home and alone.

But Dex suddenly turned off Main Street onto a side road.

"Where are we going?" she asked.

"To the beach, of course."

"Why?"

"To look at the ocean—and the stars. To see how their light glitters on the water."

"Oh, you want to take some pictures."

"Maybe."

At the end of the road, Dex pulled off into the parking area. He cut the engine and turned to her, raising his arm as though to encircle her shoulders.

She put up her hand. "No, Dex. I need to go home."

He drew back and laid his arm on the console between them. "In a while? Let's sit here a couple minutes and look at the ocean."

"All right. As long as we're just looking." She adopted a teasing tone.

When he grinned and said, "Right, just looking," her tension eased. He was an okay guy, if a little full of himself.

"I like it here," he said after a while. "I think I could live here."

"Permanently?"

"Yeah. If I had someone. The right some-one."

His gaze left the scene out the window and landed on her.

"Sometimes," she said, "the right someone is hard to find."

"You're telling me."

"And even if you thought you'd found the right person, after a while you'd want to be moving on. You'd miss the excitement of—of the rest of the world." She made a sweeping gesture.

He blew out a breath. "You're right. Here you are, meeting me only today and already you know me so well."

"Because you're just like Cody. You're soul brothers."

"And Shar?"

"Soul sister. Although I think she wants more than that with Cody." She glanced at him to measure his response.

He shook his head. "They're just good buds. She's got the hots for some guy back home. And it's obvious that Cody's interests lie elsewhere."

She drew back and studied him. "What are you saying?"

"Come on, you know how he feels about you. He's got it bad."

Luci stared. "He's told you that?"

Dex waved a hand. "Doesn't have to. It's obvious."

"But he's of the same mind you are. A 'travelin' man,' he calls himself."

"So? You can pack a suitcase, can't you?"

She shook her head. "Uh-uh. My roots are here. My family. My job. Everything I want, and everything I've worked and planned for." She added in a low voice, "Besides, he hasn't asked me."

Dex gave her a long, sober look. "Maybe he just doesn't want to hear you say no."

CHAPTER TWENTY-ONE

LUCI PULLED OPEN the door to the Willow Beach National Bank and stepped inside. After the ninety-degree temperature outside, the air-conditioning provided welcome relief. She'd come to see her father, but first she'd say hello to Don. Luci crossed the carpet to his cubicle, one of several, and peeked around the partition. He wasn't there. She approached one of the tellers.

"Hi, Alice. I'm here to see my father, but I thought I'd say hi to Don, too. Is he around?"

Alice raised her eyebrows. "You didn't know?"

"Know what?"

"He doesn't work here anymore."

"What?" Luci's raised voice turned the heads of two customers filling out forms at the island.

Alice ducked her head. "You'd better talk to your father."

"You bet I will."

Luci marched to her father's office and opened the door without knocking. He sat behind his desk talking on the phone. "No, I can't do that—" He looked up and his eyes widened. "My daughter's here. I need to go. No, it's Luci."

He hung up the phone and frowned. "What are you doing here?"

Luci stepped into the room and closed the door. "I'm not welcome here anymore?"

"Of course you are. I just didn't expect you to come around, now that you're working yourself. You could always call."

She expected him to wave her into the chair across from his desk. When he didn't, she sat anyway, perching on the edge of the seat. "I wanted to see you in person."

He picked up a pen, idly twisting it. Lines she hadn't noticed before bracketed his eyes and mouth. Where was the jovial man who used to be her father?

"What's on your mind?" he asked.

"I came to talk to you about Mom, but Alice just told me Don doesn't work here anymore, so let's talk about that first. What happened?"

"You knew he wanted to buy Ole's boat and run a charter business."

"Yes, but he doesn't have the money, and you wouldn't make him a loan. Did you change your mind?"

He tossed down the pen. "No. He and Max partnered up. That way, Don could swing it."

"What about Arliss?"

"She's not happy. He'll be gone a lot, working odd hours and not making as much money as he made here. She'll have to do something to keep them afloat."

"I can imagine how much his leaving upsets you. Are you two still speaking to each other?"

"Barely."

Luci let a couple seconds go by, and then she said, "Okay, now what about Mom? She says she'll be all right, but whenever I go home or try to talk to her on the phone, she doesn't want to talk. Has she been to see Dr. Norris?"

"Not that I know of." Erv swiveled his chair so that he could look out the window.

Luci thought her father's response odd. Wouldn't he know whether his wife had seen a doctor or not? "Don't you think she should?"

"That's up to her."

Luci shook her head. "Don't you care about her anymore?"

He swung back around and faced her again. "Of course I do," he said, slamming his fist on the desk. "Why would you say a thing like that?"

"I don't know. Our family is falling apart. Next, you'll be telling me something about Francine and Will."

He picked up his pen again. "They may be splitting up."

Luci sagged back in her chair. "I don't believe this."

"I shouldn't have said anything. Fran has a chance to be associate broker, but she'll have to move to Oceanside. Will doesn't want to go. He says he and the kids never see her anyway, and he likes his job at the marina."

"And she would leave them?"

"Your sister is ambitious. And smart. I probably should have steered her into banking and let Don do his fishing."

"You had it all planned out for us, didn't you?"

He lifted his chin. "I don't see what's wrong with encouraging one's children to be successful."

"Nothing is wrong with that, as long as you let them decide exactly what constitutes success."

Her dad sat forward. "Are you lecturing me? Is that why you came here? To give me a lesson on how to be a husband and a father? Well, let me tell you something, Luci, you wouldn't have that prestigious job at the chamber if it wasn't for your good old dad and his connections."

His words hit Luci like a punch in the stomach. And yet, hadn't she suspected that all along? She'd ignored the hints. Now, her father had confirmed the truth. She hadn't landed the job on her own merits; Glen had hired her because he owed Erv a favor. Her stomach churned. Fearing she would be sick, she jumped up and ran out the door.

Back at the chamber office, Luci slumped at her desk. She turned on her computer but only stared blankly at the screen. Thank goodness Tessa wasn't there, so she didn't have to put on a show of business as usual.

She finally opened a file and typed a few

words, but when she read them over, they didn't make much sense and she pressed the delete key.

She stood and walked to the window. In the courtyard, the fountain burbled, and the surrounding flowers formed a ring of bright colors. Several people were strolling, while others sat on the wrought-iron benches.

She turned away and surveyed her office. Returning to Willow Beach and her family and landing this job had fulfilled a long-held dream. Now, that dream had turned into a nightmare.

ON THURSDAY, LUCI'S father called. "We need to have a family meeting," he said.

"Dinner on Sunday?" she asked, allowing a hopeful note to creep into her voice.

"No, not dinner. Friday evening. I'll expect you then."

"All right, but what's this about?"

"Just be there, Luci. Seven o'clock."

On Friday, at six forty-five, Luci pulled into the driveway at her parents' home. She parked next to Don's SUV and Will's truck. As she stepped from her car, Francine drove up in her company vehicle with the Talbot Realty logo on the door.

"Do you know what this meeting is about?" Luci asked after she and Francine exchanged greetings and a hug.

"I have an idea." Francine slipped her keys into her shoulder bag.

"Is it Mom? Is she really sick?"

Francine shook her head. "Better you hear it from them."

The kitchen was dark, without the aromas of cooking that always greeted Luci when she came for Sunday dinner. But then, this wasn't Sunday, and they weren't having dinner.

She and Fran continued on to the screened porch, where the others were gathered. Hands clasped behind his back, head down, Erv paced in front of the glass wall overlooking the yard and Anna's garden. Anna sat on a wicker sofa, with Don next to her. Arliss and Will sat nearby. Arliss's eyes were sad, and Will's forehead was wrinkled with uncertainty.

Luci and Francine each leaned down to kiss Anna's cheek. Although her lips smiled, her eyes were red and watery.

"Hey, you two," Don said.

"I heard about your job transition," Luci said. She wanted to add, *What were you thinking?* but didn't.

"Yeah, well, it's something I've always wanted to do."

Luci's father stopped pacing. "Now that everyone's here…"

"Where are the children?" Luci asked, looking around.

"I thought it best they not be present for this," Erv said.

"Our neighbor is watching them," Arliss put in.

"Sit down, Luci, Francine." Erv pointed to vacant chairs. "This is the hardest thing I've ever had to do," he began when they were seated. "And I want you to know that if I could, I would spare you." His gaze passed over them, landing on Anna.

She bit her lip and looked away.

Erv continued, "As I feared, the rumors around town are starting."

"Rumors?" Luci asked. "What rumors?"

"Just listen," Francine said.

"This concerns Helen Stevens and her grandson, Jason," Erv said.

Helen Stevens. Jason. Luci searched her memory.

"…at the sand-castle contest," Erv was saying.

Okay, now she remembered. The sad-looking woman who walked with a cane and the little boy who loved airplanes.

"You all met them that day. Well, you didn't, Francine."

"I know who you're talking about," Francine said. "She lives in Oceanside. I've seen her there."

"Not lives," Erv corrected. "She's staying with a friend who lives there, Mavis Cook. Helen is from California." He paused and rubbed the back of his neck. "Anyway, the boy, Jason…" He walked back to the glass wall and returned to stand in front of them.

Luci wished he'd sit down. His pacing put her more on edge than she already was.

"Get to it, would you?" Don said. "You're not at the bank talking to one of your customers."

Luci held her breath, waiting for her father's comeback, which would surely start an argument between father and son. Instead, Erv sucked in a breath and said, "Helen's grandson... Jason. He, ah, he's my grandson, too."

What? She must have heard wrong. She looked around at the others. No one said anything, but no one seemed particularly surprised, either. They must have heard the rumors.

"Are you sure?" she asked.

"Yes. There's no doubt in my mind."

"How? When?" Luci asked. The others might not care, but she had to know.

Erv ran a hand through his hair. "Yes, you deserve a few of the details."

"A few?" Luci sputtered. "You spring something like this on us, and you're not going to tell us the whole story?"

"You must know how painful this is for me," Erv said.

"Painful for you? What about us? Your family."

"Okay, okay." Erv spread his hands. "If you'll calm down, I'll tell you more."

He looked at the floor. "After Francine was born, your mother and I went through some rough times. I had a degree in business, but my job didn't pay very much. Anna didn't want to leave Willow Beach or your grandparents. And I understood that, but I kept telling her that if we moved back to California, where I was from, I could get a better job."

"So this is Mother's fault?" Luci said.

"Be quiet, Luci," Francine said. "And just listen for a change."

"And so we decided to separate," Erv continued. "Anna, Don and Francine went to live with her parents, and I went back to California. I landed a job at a bank. It was entry-level as a teller, and didn't pay much, but to me it was better than, say, working at the grocery store."

"Or being a fishing boat captain," Don said.

Erv shot him a look. "Yes, that, too," he said with a touch of defiance. "Anyway, while I was in California, I went to a college class reunion. Helen was there. We'd gone out a few times as undergrads. Nothing serious between us. Not on my part, anyway. After graduation, she'd headed to LA for a screen test, which landed her a role in a movie. At the same time, I'd met Anna when she and some girlfriends came to California on a vacation."

Luci glanced at her mother. Tears were

rolling down her cheeks. Francine leaned over to hand her a tissue, and Don tightened his arm around her shoulders.

"You've all heard the rest of that story," Erv said. "Anna and I fell in love and married and settled here in Willow Beach. Anyway, back to the college reunion. Helen and I, ah, got together, just one time—"

"I don't want to hear this." Luci stuck her hands over her ears.

Her father frowned. "A few minutes ago, you insisted on hearing all of it, Luci. Make up your mind. Or, leave the room." He gestured to the door.

Luci dropped her arms. Covering her ears hadn't blocked out his voice, anyway.

Erv took a deep breath. "All the time I was in Cal, I knew I still loved Anna. I missed her and my kids—yes, even you, Don," Erv said with a bit of mock humor. "And so I quit my job, came back here and we reconciled. I told her I'd live here or anywhere she wanted, as long as we could be together. I wanted my family back. A job opened up at the bank, which I was lucky enough to get, and then Luci came along—and here we are."

"What happened to Helen?" Arliss asked.

Luci was glad someone else had spoken up, so she didn't have to ask all the questions.

"I never heard from her again," Erv said, "until last month. She showed up at the bank one day, said she was visiting a friend in Oceanside. I took her out for a cup of coffee, and that's when she told me about Jason. She wanted me to come to her friend's house and meet him. Which I did."

"But if he's your grandson, there must be…"

"A son or daughter," Erv finished. "Yes." He looked down and his voice dropped. "There was a son, Brian."

"Was?"

"He and his wife were killed in a traffic accident several years ago when Jason was three."

Arliss pressed her fingers to her lips. "A son you never knew about? I can't imagine."

"No, I never knew about him," Erv said, sadness lacing his voice.

"Why didn't she tell you about Brian— before?" Luci asked.

"Because I had already come back here and reconciled with your mother. Helen knew that I loved Anna and wanted to be with my family. She knew how important family was—and still is—to me. So, she raised Brian on her own."

Francine narrowed her eyes. "Are you sure Jason is your grandson?"

"Yes, I had a DNA test done. I didn't want to, because I believed Helen, but she insisted."

"So what does she want from you now?" Arliss asked.

"Money, I bet." Francine nodded and folded her arms. "Why else would she be here?"

"That's all that matters to you, isn't it, Fran? Money," Will said. His bitter tone shocked Luci. She'd always known him to be easygoing and good-natured.

Francine glared at him. "Somebody has to pay the bills."

Erv raised both hands. "Please, we've got enough going on here without you two arguing."

"Sorry," Will mumbled.

"Helen doesn't want money," Erv went on. "She wants Jason to know his family. To know me, his grandfather. We're his only relations. Brian's wife was an Afghani woman he met while he was in the army. She has no relatives that Helen ever knew of."

"She's not going to move here, is she?" Francine said.

"No, not now, anyway. But her friend, Mavis, has said she and Jason can visit whenever they want to."

"She was an actress?" Arliss said. "I've never heard of her." She shrugged and looked around at the others.

"She started out acting and then went into set designing and other backstage work," Erv said. "She's retired now—on disability."

"What's wrong with her?" Don asked.

"I'm not sure," Erv said. "She didn't want to talk about it."

"Could be an act," Francine said, and then, when everyone groaned she added, "Well, you said she was an actress."

In the silence that followed, Luci looked at Anna. "Mom, you haven't said a word. Is this why you've been having headaches?"

"I don't know," Anna said, not meeting Luci's eyes. "Maybe."

Luci turned back to her father. "What are you going to do now, Dad?"

"When the occasion arises, I'm going to

be a grandfather to Jason. And continue to be here for all of you—my family."

Luci burst into a fit of hysterical laughter.

"What's so funny?" Don demanded.

"Dad calling us a family, that's what's funny. We're not a family. Not anymore. We haven't been since I came back, but our disintegration probably began a long time before that."

No one said anything. Luci's laughter died away. Tears blurring her eyes, she jumped up and ran out the door. No one tried to stop her.

CHAPTER TWENTY-TWO

CODY READ THE email again, excitement surging through his veins. A job offer. Not just any job offer, but one promising all sorts of adventures. As photographer for an archaeological expedition in Peru, he'd be in on the discoveries as well as have time to explore the countryside and take all the photos he wanted.

Then he thought about leaving Luci. His joy faded and a dull ache invaded his chest.

He didn't want to leave her. He was in love with her. Exactly when that had happened, he wasn't sure. But it had. Big-time. He was certain she was in love with him, too. Not the crush she'd had when she was in high school, but full-blown, mature love.

Although no words had passed between them, he knew. The way she looked at him with longing. The way she responded when he kissed her. The way she nestled close to him when they danced.

Yes, she wanted to stay here with her family and her job. But if you loved someone, you'd make sacrifices to be with that person, wouldn't you? And he'd make sacrifices for her, too. The archaeological dig was for six months. After that, they'd work out something they'd both be happy with.

Cody stared at the email message again. What about this job? He needed to give them an answer. An idea occurred to him, and he snapped his fingers. There was a way he could accept this job and be with Luci, too. He tapped in his reply.

The following day, the director of the expedition answered his query. Yes, it just so happened they were looking for a writer, and Cody's wife was welcome to apply for the position. Cody made a fist and pumped the air.

Wife. He sobered a bit as he let the word and the concept sink in. He'd thought it would be a long time before he had a wife. Now, after a couple of months back in Willow Beach, back with *Luci*, all that had changed. Yet, he knew this was what he wanted.

Now he had to propose, which created a

whole new set of problems. For starters, he needed a ring. Not wanting to risk any gossip that might reach Luci before he did, he nixed purchasing it locally at Crown Jewels and instead went to a store in Oceanside. He wished she was with him, but he did the best he could to pick out a ring set he thought she would like.

Back at home, he placed the ring box on the table, took out his phone and speed-dialed Luci's number. When she came on the line, her voice sounded thick, as though she had a cold. "You okay?" he asked.

"Ah, yeah, I'm…okay."

"Something's wrong, I can tell."

"Never mind. Why are you calling? It's Saturday. Why aren't you out with Dex and Shar?"

"They've gone. They both got assignments and wanted to visit their families again before starting work. They said to tell you bye and that they enjoyed meeting you."

"They got assignments? So, you did, too, right?"

"Yes, I did. In fact, that's what I want to talk to you about." This wasn't going at all the way he'd planned. "How about dinner tomorrow? Since you're not doing your family dinners, we could go out instead."

"No, thanks, Cody. I don't feel like going out."

"Then I'll come over tonight—unless you're busy."

"Not busy. But I don't think—"

"I'll bring dinner. Something you'll like. C'mon, Luci… I really need to see you. It's important."

She sighed. "Okay, but I can't promise to be good company."

Two hours later, Cody rang Luci's doorbell. He held a large take-out box from Beach Café, where he'd purchased a crab salad for Luci and a burger for him. Not the fancy dinner he'd planned for his proposal, but it would have to do. The ring was in his jacket pocket, along with information about the expedition and other details of what would be their new life together. He hoped. Now that the moment was almost upon him, he was a little shaky inside.

Luci answered the door. "Hey, Cody." She offered him a weak smile.

"Ready for your favorite salad from the Beach Café?" He handed her the box.

She opened it and peeked inside. "Crab salad? That's so thoughtful of you. Come in."

They fixed plates and took them out to the patio, where they watched the waves splash the shore and the clouds drift by and the birds swoop, all the while making small talk about everything and nothing. She only picked at her salad, finally putting down her fork and saying, "I'll save the rest of this for tomorrow."

"You're hurting, Luci. Want to talk about it?"

She looked away. "I don't know. It's—it's a mess."

"Glen giving you fits?"

She waved a hand. "No, not any more than usual. It's my family, although I don't know why I'm still calling them that. We're not acting like a family—more like strangers on the street."

"Hey, that's pretty extreme."

"Yeah, well, last night, Dad told us he has—guess what?—a grandson no one knew about. Not even him."

Cody put down his fork and stared. "What?"

"That woman who was at the sand-castle

contest with the little boy. You met her in Oceanside, you said. It seems she and my father, well, you get the picture."

"Oh, yeah. Helen and Erv."

She sat straight. "You knew about this, too? Did everyone in town know about what my father did besides me?"

He held up both hands. "I didn't know for sure, but I had my suspicions. I saw them together in a café in Oceanside, and I talked to her at the kids' park one day when I was there. She said she was an old friend of his."

"Why didn't you tell me?"

"I had no proof there was anything between them, and it wasn't my place to speculate about your father. But, if anything, I wanted to protect you."

She frowned. "I'm not sure that's protecting me. I was so caught off guard."

"Why don't you tell me the whole story?"

"Are you sure you want to hear it?"

"Of course. We're friends, aren't we?" And so much more, he wanted to add. But the time wasn't right to bring up the other reason he'd come tonight. She was hurting now. Big-time. He needed to be there for her.

He stood, picked up his plate and reached for hers. "I'll put these in the sink while you grab a jacket. Then we'll walk and talk."

"Well...all right."

While he cleaned up the kitchen, she grabbed a jacket and tied a scarf around her hair. They left the apartment, walking through the dunes and the soft sand to the hard-packed sand near the surf. The sun perched on the horizon. By the time she'd finished the whole sorry story, the sun had long disappeared and a couple stars had popped out.

He put his arm around her and drew her close. "I'm sorry, Luci. Tough stuff going on for you."

She rested her head against his shoulder and gave a soft sigh. "Thanks for letting me vent."

"Anytime."

"We'd better be getting back."

He kept her hand in his as they retraced their steps. He slipped his other hand into his jacket pocket and grasped the ring box. Was now the time?

"You've had some bad shocks," he began.

"But I'm betting everything will work out." Oh, man, that was lame. Couldn't he do better?

"I don't know," she said. "But one thing's for sure."

"What's that?"

"No matter how angry I might be, I won't abandon them."

"Were you, ah, considering that? Moving away…or something?"

"A lot of possibilities have been going through my mind."

"Maybe getting away would be best for you. Give them time to figure things out for themselves."

She shook her head. "No, my place is here in Willow Beach. More so now than ever before. They need me."

"But—" He clamped his jaw shut, knowing any further argument would be futile.

"What?" she asked. "What were you about to say?"

"Nothing." He opened his fingers and let the ring box drop to the bottom of his pocket.

LATER THAT EVENING, as Luci was brushing her teeth, she realized Cody had never told her about his assignment. That was her fault. She'd monopolized their time together with her problems. He'd understood, too, and taking him into her confidence had relieved her stress. Well, she'd hear about his new assignment next week at work. And then he'd be gone.

What would it be like to travel around the world, free and unencumbered by responsibility? She recalled their day trip and his wanting to give her a glimpse of his life. She had to admit the outing had been fun, offering the spontaneity she rarely allowed herself. Would she be able to live that way?

But what did it matter, when he hadn't asked her to share his life. No, that was not part of his plan. Or hers, either.

After a restless night, she was back to brooding over her family and their problems. She still had unanswered questions. Luci wished she could talk to Helen Stevens and hear her side of the story. The more she thought about it, the more the idea took hold. But, even if she could contact Helen, would Helen be willing to talk to her?

There was only one way to find out. Helen and Jason were staying with a friend in Oceanside. Her father had mentioned the friend's name. Mavis something. Mavis Cook, that was it.

Luckily, Mavis Cook was listed in the Oceanside phone directory. When Mavis answered Luci's call, Luci identified herself and asked if she could speak to Helen. A few seconds later, Helen came on the line, and two hours later, Luci pulled up in front of Mavis Cook's modest frame home. She sat there a minute staring at the front door, her stomach churning. Did she really want to do this? What could she possibly gain by talking to Helen Stevens?

Helen answered the door. "Come in," she said, stepping back to admit Luci.

Limping and leaning on her cane, Helen led Luci along a hallway to a living room dominated by a brick fireplace. She scooped up a picture book and a couple of toy airplanes from a chair and dropped them into a box at one end of the fireplace. "Jason's not real good about picking up his toys," she said and then gestured to the chairs and sofa. "Sit down wherever you like."

Luci chose the sofa, and Helen eased into a chair across from her, propping her cane against the seat. The scent from a bowl of roses on the coffee table reached Luci's nose, reminding her of her mother. "Where is your grandson?" she asked.

"He and Mavis went shopping. They'll be back soon." For a couple seconds, they stared at each other, and then Helen said, "So Erv told you about me and Jason."

Luci straightened her spine. "Yes, and I want to know why you came here. Why now? You never told him about his son. All those years…why not just leave it that way?" She swallowed hard against the anger and indignation welling up inside. "But, no, you had to come here and…and break up our family."

"I might have upset your family, but, according to Erv, you were already having problems."

"He told you our personal business?"

"Erv and I are old friends."

Luci squeezed her eyes shut. She didn't want to think about that.

"But you asked me a question that I will try to answer. I don't know if coming here was the right thing to do. I only know I always felt so guilty because I'd never told Erv about Brian, or him about Erv. Father and son, and they never knew each other. How sad is that?"

Helen pulled a cell phone from her skirt pocket. She swiped the screen and then handed the phone to Luci. "This is Brian."

Dressed in his army uniform, a smile on his face, Brian stood tall and proud. Luci gasped. "Except for his dark hair, he looks like Don. They have the same smile, the same straight nose."

"Yes, that's what I thought when I met your brother."

"And Brian's our half brother. I never thought of that." A lump formed in Luci's throat.

"Yes, that's right. You're related to him, too." Helen gestured to the phone. "There are more pictures. Keep scrolling."

Luci complied and by the time she'd reached the end of them, she'd seen several more of Brian, some with his wife and some of their son, Jason.

"His wife was very pretty." She gazed at a photo of the petite, dark-eyed woman.

"Her name was Delara," Helen said. "It means 'beloved' in her language."

Luci looked up. "Dad said they were killed in an accident."

Helen's eyes clouded. "They were on a ski trip. Brian loved to ski and wanted to teach Delara. Jason was too young to go, so I took care of him. They were driving on a mountain pass. It was snowing, and a truck jackknifed, setting off a chain reaction of collisions. Brian and Delara's car went through the guardrail and over the cliff."

Luci put her hand to her throat. "How awful. I'm so sorry." She let a few moments pass and then handed back the phone. "What did Brian think happened to his father?"

"When he was old enough to ask, I told him his dad had died before he was born." She sighed as she laid the phone on the coffee table. "But that didn't chase away my guilt."

"Why didn't you tell Erv about Brian?"

"Because I knew how much he loved Anna and his children. His family. I didn't want to risk him losing what he loved because of what had happened between us."

"Didn't you think it would upset him to learn about Jason?"

She twisted her hands in her lap. "I worry

so much about Jason. I'm all he has now and as you can see, I'm not in the best of health."

"What happened to you? If I may ask."

"Of course. I was an actress for a while, but later gave that up to work behind the scenes. One day, a huge pile of bricks toppled over onto me. Two surgeries on my shattered hip, and I still can't walk normally and without pain. The doctors want another go at it, but I don't know about that. The accident forced me into disability retirement. Luckily, I have enough money for me and Jason to get along."

"Francine thinks that's why you came here. To ask Erv for money."

Helen shook her head. "Erv said she tends to be cynical. But, no, I wouldn't take it even if he offered."

"Then what? Do you want my father and mother to take Jason and raise him?"

Helen stared at her in horror and pressed a hand to her chest. "Oh, my, no. I would never give him up. I told you, I just wanted him to know his family."

Luci struggled to keep her voice level. "But he's too young to understand the relationship between him and my father."

"He understands what 'grandfather' means, and that's the main thing. The truth can come later."

Luci pressed her lips together. "We're not the perfect family you may have thought us to be. In fact, there's not much family left. My parents aren't getting along. Francine plans to leave Will. Don and my father aren't speaking because Don quit the bank to run a charter-fishing business. So far, his marriage seems intact, but who knows how long that will last? Arliss is a patient woman, but everyone has a breaking point."

Helen nodded. "I heard about everyone's troubles, and I'm sorry. But I know your father really loves your mother, and I'm sure she loves him, too. I believe they'll all work out their problems. Love will win out."

"What makes you so sure? Did you love my father when—when—oh, never mind, I don't really want to know."

"I want to tell you about that time," Helen said. "I've been thinking a lot about what happened then. And I realize that what I felt for your father, initially, was a crush."

A crush? Luci leaned closer.

"He was on the football team, and I was

flattered when he paid attention to me. We went out a few times. When we met at the reunion, there I was, back in college again with my crush on the big football player."

"How did you know it wasn't love?"

Helen smiled. "Love takes time to develop. It's more than looking at the other person with stars in your eyes and thinking he's perfect. Love is knowing he's not perfect and caring for him, anyway. Love is sharing your life, the good and the bad. It's making sacrifices to be with each other."

"Wow. To know all that, you must have experienced it."

"Oh, I did. I met a man later in life, and we fell in love."

"What happened? Where is he? Did you marry him?"

"We were engaged, but before we could get married, he died of a heart attack. Brian was ten at the time. We would have been a nice family." Her smile turned wistful.

"I'm sorry you lost your true love," Luci said, wrapping her arms around herself. "But I'm still upset."

"I know you are, Luci. And I understand that you're worried about your family."

"I thought we were all so happy together. I couldn't wait to come back to Willow Beach and be with them."

"Family is important. I know your dad thinks so, because when he was separated from Anna and Don and Francine, he was really very unhappy."

"Then why is no one happy now?"

Helen looked thoughtful for a moment and then said in a quiet voice, "Do you think maybe you're expecting too much of them? You want everything to be perfect, but life just isn't. And people aren't perfect, either. Goals change. Lifestyles change."

Luci stared at her hands lying in her lap. "I hate to see everyone so at odds with each other, the way we have been since I came back."

"That would upset me, too. But maybe you should let them work things out among themselves and, well, move on with your own life." She waved a hand. "I know, I'm a fine one to tell you how to run your life, but don't neglect your young man."

Luci frowned. "My young man? Who are you talking about?"

"Why, Cody, the man you were with at the sand-castle contest."

"Cody and I aren't dating…"

"Well, it's obvious he cares for you a great deal, and you for him. I could tell by the way you looked at each other."

"We're just friends. Besides, he's leaving soon to take another job."

Helen pressed her fingers to her lips. "Oh, my. Are you sure you want to let him get away?"

Before Luci could answer, the front door opened and closed, and she heard footsteps and voices in the hallway.

Jason burst into the room. "Grandma, Grandma, look at the airplane Mavis bought me." Holding up a toy airplane, he ran to Helen.

"That was nice of her, dear." Helen put her arm around him, brushed back his hair and kissed his forehead. "We have company." Holding his slim shoulders, she turned him around to face Luci. "You met Luci at the sand-castle contest. She's your grandfather Erv's daughter."

"Hello, Jason," Luci said.

Jason clutched his toy airplane to his chest. "Hi, Luci. I remember you."

"And this is my friend, Mavis." Helen nodded toward a tall, gray-haired woman, who had come into the room behind Jason.

"Welcome, Luci." Mavis peeked over the top of the brown paper bag she carried. "I've heard a lot about you... All good," she added with a laugh. "Well, I'd better get these groceries put away." She left the room and headed down the hallway.

While they'd been talking, Jason had skipped over to his toy box and retrieved two more airplanes. He was lining them up with his new one on the carpet.

"I'm gonna be a pilot when I grow up," he said.

Luci leaned forward. "In the army?"

His brow wrinkled. "I don't know yet. Maybe. My dad was in the army," he added with a note of pride. "Anyways, want to see the rest of my planes?"

"Well, I—" She glanced at Helen.

"Stay awhile longer, if you can," Helen said. "We'll have tea."

"All right."

While Helen went to see about the tea,

Jason lifted another toy airplane from the box, chattering about the wingspan. He handed the plane to Luci. She inspected it and handed it back, and soon an array of planes lined the carpet.

"Here's something else I like." Instead of another plane, he pulled a picture book from the box.

"Watch Me Fly," she said. "I remember this book from when I was a kid."

"Yeah, Grandma says it's an old story."

"But it's a good story, about a toy airplane that learns to fly."

"Uh-huh. Can you read it to me? I can read most of the words, but some are hard."

"Sure. Come sit by me." She patted the place beside her on the sofa.

They had just finished the story when Helen and Mavis came in with the tea and cookies.

"Jason loves books almost as much as airplanes." Helen handed Luci a mug of sweet-smelling tea.

They talked about children's books as they drank their tea and ate the chocolate chip cookies. After a while, Luci looked at her watch. "I'd better be going. I didn't mean to stay so long."

"I'm glad you did." Helen put her mug on the tray. "We've had a chance to get to know each other, and you to know Jason." The boy was sitting on the floor, playing with his airplanes.

Luci picked up her purse and stood. "What are you going to do now?"

"Jason and I are returning to California soon." Helen grasped her cane and stood, ready to accompany Luci to the front door.

"But I told her she's welcome to come stay with me anytime," Mavis put in.

"So, we'll see," Helen said.

Luci wasn't about to make any promises, especially promises that weren't hers to make. However, when Jason ran over and said "Bye, Luci," she leaned down and gave him a hug.

Luci said, "Why don't you call me 'Aunt Luci'?"

His face broke into a grin. "Okay… Aunt Luci."

Luci's eyes were moist as she drove away from Mavis Cook's house and caught the highway leading back to Willow Beach. Even though she still didn't agree with what Helen had done, she had a better understanding of why she'd done it.

CHAPTER TWENTY-THREE

CODY CHECKED THE contents of his backpack, making sure he had everything he needed. He zipped the pack and set it on the floor next to his duffel bag, the only other luggage he was taking on this trip. He'd long ago learned to travel light.

In just a couple hours, his mom and Mel would take him to catch the bus to Tacoma, where he would ride a shuttle to Sea Tac airport. Then he'd board a flight to LAX and from there to Lima, Peru, where he'd join the archaeological expedition.

Last week, he'd helped Luci finish a batch of the brochures, taking a few pictures that were still needed. He'd finally had the opportunity to tell her about his upcoming trip. She'd asked a few questions and told him she was happy for him but seemed preoccupied. He said goodbye to Glen, thanking him for the job, and Glen had assured him that when they needed a photographer, he was at the top of the list.

Cody had also gone on a last fishing trip with Don and Max in their newly acquired boat and had dinner with Sylvie and Ben.

And now he'd said goodbye to everyone but Luci. The question was, how exactly to do that. Should he talk to her while they were alone, or while others were around? If he arranged for them to be alone, he might break down and reveal his true feelings.

At their last meeting, without even knowing he'd come to propose, she'd made it clear she had no intention of abandoning her family. He respected her loyalty. He just wished that somehow her loyalty included him.

He finally decided to say goodbye at the chamber's office. That was where they'd started their association this summer, and it seemed appropriate to end it there, as well. Thankfully, Tessa was on an errand, Glen was out of the office, too, and Marge was busy working on a display in the hallway.

He'd expected to find Luci typing away at her computer or sitting at the worktable. Instead, she stood at the window looking out at the courtyard.

He crossed the room to stand beside her.

"Hey, Luci," he said.

"Hello, Cody."

He tried to read her smile. Sad? Happy? Wistful? He couldn't tell. Maybe all of the above.

"I just stopped in to—"

She nodded. "To say goodbye. I know. When are you leaving?"

"Tomorrow."

She turned back to the window. "Well. Have a good trip."

"Luci, I—"

"I think the only thing left is to say goodbye."

He stared at the floor. "Yeah, sure. So—ah, let's have a hug, then, okay?"

"Of course."

Holding her in his arms was almost his undoing. He wanted to tell her how much he loved her and crush her lips with his kisses. He wanted to carry her away with him and never let her go.

Instead, he kissed her cheek and said, "You take care, Luci."

"I will. You, too, Cody."

In the doorway, he stopped and turned

around, but Luci had already put her back toward him. She was looking out the window again, her shoulders set.

BACK AT HIS APARTMENT, Cody sighed. His mom and Mel would be here any minute, but he knew now that he didn't want those words to be the last they said to each other. There was so much more to say, so much he wanted to tell her.

On impulse, he pulled out his phone and called her. No answer. He sent her a text. No answer. He paced the room. Looked at his watch. *Call her again, leave a voice mail.* And say what? *I love you? Marry me and come with me?* No, she belonged here. Next time he saw her—if there were a next time— she'd be hooked up with someone, a nester, someone who'd put down roots as deep and as permanent as hers.

A knock sounded on his door. Luci? Hope surged in his chest. He flung open the door.

Mel stood there. "Time to hit the road."

"Yeah." Cody slung on his backpack, picked up his duffel bag, turned out the light and followed Mel down the driveway.

ON WEDNESDAY MORNING, Luci entered her office, as usual. But instead of sitting down at her desk and turning on her computer, she stood in the middle of the room and looked around. At the beginning of summer, the table in front of the windows had been piled high with work to be done. Now it had only a couple small stacks of paper. The filing cabinet had been cleaned out and organized. The bulletin board displayed the poster for the sand-castle contest and the latest newsletter. On her desk were copies of *Coastal Living* containing her articles. A lump formed in her throat. She'd been so proud of landing this job.

Yet, nothing in her life was what she'd believed it to be. Not her job. Not her family. Not Cody.

Cody.

Just thinking about him brought an ache to her heart. By now, he was in LA, ready to hop the plane to Peru. Well, that was for the best. She had to learn to live her life without him.

She took a last look around her office and then walked out. She approached Marge at her desk. "Is Glen in his office?"

Marge looked up from her monitor and frowned. "He is, but he's in a bad mood."

"I'll talk to him anyway."

Luci marched to Glen's open door and looked in. He sat at his desk, his back to her, gazing out the window. She knocked on the doorjamb.

He whirled his chair around. When he saw her, the crease between his brows deepened. "What? I've got six things going here. Can it wait?"

Luci lifted her chin and stepped into his office. "This will take only a minute."

"Guess I shoulda closed my door," he grumbled.

He didn't offer her a seat, but she would've remained standing anyway.

She took a deep breath and got right to the point. "Glen, I'm turning in my resignation."

He dropped his jaw. "What? Why? I know you've had some problems with Tessa, but she'll be going back to school soon."

"I'm not leaving because of Tessa."

"What, then? You get a better offer someplace else?"

Luci folded her arms. "No, I'm leaving be-cause I know you gave me this job not because of my qualifications, but as a favor to my father. He told you to hire me, and you did."

He shrugged. "A lot of people get jobs through referrals. It's done all the time."

"This was more than a referral."

"So what? You got a job, and that's what you wanted, isn't it? What's the problem?"

"I want a job on my own merits. Not because my boss owes my father a favor."

He shook his head. "What am I supposed to tell people? What am I supposed to tell Erv? He'll think I was too hard on you."

"I'm sure he knows why I'm doing this."

"Then what are you going to do?"

"I don't know."

"Aren't many jobs for writers in this town. I suppose you could freelance for Eva and Mark at the *Herald*, but that wouldn't put much money in your pocket."

"That's not your worry. I'll stay till you find a replacement."

He made a dismissive wave. "You don't have to stay. Marge can fill in until I find someone else. She was filling in when you came."

Luci went back to her office and began

cleaning out her desk. A few minutes later, Tessa arrived.

"Uncle Glen told me you're quitting," she said.

"That's right." Luci tossed some papers into the wastebasket.

"Why? Because of me? I'm going back to school soon."

Luci stopped and faced Tessa. "No, not because of you. I decided this job isn't what I want, after all." True enough.

Tessa's mouth turned down. "I don't want you to leave. I want you to be here when I come back next summer. I'm sorry I was such a bad assistant. You were right—I wanted you to complain to Uncle Glen so he would get mad and let me go. But then, I started to like the job. Well, most of it. Some things were always boring."

Luci had to smile. "You'll make a good assistant for the next person, Tessa. Just remember what you learned this summer."

"All right… But I still wish you weren't leaving."

Tessa helped Luci box up her personal belongings. They exchanged hugs and good lucks, and then Luci left. On the way out,

Marge gave her a hug, too, and they promised to keep in touch and get together for lunch.

LUCI STOOD AT her patio door looking out at the beach, glad to see the sunshine. The past few days had been cloudy and rainy, which matched her mood. After quitting her job, she'd experienced some near panicky moments wondering if she had done the right thing. Finally, she decided she had and made her peace with her choice.

She didn't call anyone in her family to tell them. She'd no doubt they'd heard the news, anyway. Her father didn't call, but she hadn't expected him to. Arliss phoned, though, expressing sympathy that Luci's dream job hadn't worked out. Francine texted her, assuring Luci she was available if Luci wanted to "process her decision." Whatever that meant.

Her mother called, too, her voice full of worry. "Sometimes, when we're not feeling good we make decisions we come to regret," she said, and Luci wondered if she weren't speaking of herself.

In the meantime, the rain hadn't kept Luci off the beach. She'd put on her raincoat and vinyl hat and plowed through the wet sand.

But somehow, beach walking didn't work its usual magic. By the fourth day, she gave herself a kick. She'd felt sorry for herself long enough. Luci recalled what Helen had said about letting the family work out their problems and moving on with her own life, and decided she was right.

She purchased copies of the *Willow Beach Herald*, the *Oceanside Observer* and the *Seattle Times*. Yes, she'd go to Seattle, if need be. She'd find a job somewhere. Her life might not be the vision of perfection she'd imagined. But it was hers, and she was going to take charge of it starting now.

And now that the sun was shining brightly, she had new hope and a new resolve. Wearing her favorite straw hat and armed with the help wanted ads, Luci headed once again for the beach. After a short walk, she settled in her favorite spot among the driftwood logs. For a while, she gazed at the waves rolling in and breaking on the shore, the people jogging and walking, the birds flapping and cawing, all so familiar. And yet different. Or was she the one who had changed?

She turned her attention to the newspapers, looking first at the ads in the *Herald*. Not much there. Fuller's Foods needed a checker and the Beach Café a waitperson. Oceanside offered more, but nothing that caught her eye. She turned to the *Seattle Times*. Seattle was probably where she would land. Well, having gone to university there, she was familiar with the city. Living there wouldn't be so bad.

A shadow fell across the sand. She'd been so absorbed in her want-ad search she hadn't noticed anyone's approach. When she looked up from under her straw hat, her eyes widened.

"Cody! What are you doing here? I thought you were leaving town. What happened?"

He dropped down beside her. His sudden nearness sent her heartbeat into overdrive.

"I got as far as LA and then realized I'd forgotten something. Something important."

"One of your cameras, I suppose."

"No…and I'm not even wearing one today."

Sure enough, there wasn't a camera slung around his neck.

"I can't believe you'd go anywhere without a camera."

He looked a bit sheepish. "Okay, it's in the

car, which is parked back at your place. But, hey, one step at a time, right?"

She had to laugh. But then she sobered again and asked, "So what does this all mean?"

He moved closer and put his arm around her shoulders. "It means there's just you and me and nothing between us. I don't want anything to be between us, ever. Not a job, not family, nothing. I need you in my life, Luci. I have for a long, long time.

"I told you I took the job at the chamber because I needed money. That was true. But a stronger, deeper reason was that I wanted to spend time with you again. Only I wouldn't admit it. And then, I started to fall for you—but I was afraid of commitment."

"And you're not now?"

"No. You're what I want."

"But what about all the traveling you want to do? Seeing the world."

He ran a finger down her cheek, smoothing a curl behind her ear. "My world is wherever you are."

"But I don't know where I'm going. I quit my job."

"I know. I stopped at the chamber before

coming here. And I don't know where I'm going, either. Why don't we hang up a map and throw a dart?"

She shook her head. "Cody, Cody. That is so you. Crazy you."

"But you love me, anyway, crazy or not?"

"I do love you, Cody." Luci raised her voice and let the wind carry the words. "I love you. Wow, that felt good. I've wanted to say that for *so* long."

"I love you, too, Luci. But before we decide where we're going to land, let's seal the deal." He reached into his jacket pocket and drew out a ring box. He opened the box and held it out. "Like it?"

Luci gazed in awe at the diamond encircled with emeralds. "Yes, it's beautiful."

"Luci Monroe, will you marry me?"

She met his gaze, and the love shining there took her breath away. "Yes, Cody, I will marry you."

Cody slipped the ring on her finger and then cupped her face with both hands. She closed her eyes and waited in eager anticipation for the touch of his lips. He kissed her lightly at first and then wrapped his arms around her, drew her close and deepened the kiss. She put her arms around his neck and gave herself up to all the wonderful sensations the kiss evoked. Excitement. Desire. Warmth. And, most of all, love—pure love.

When he finally ended the kiss, they both were breathless. He touched her forehead with his. "I can't believe it."

"What?"

"What I've been missing all these years."

"I wasn't ready, either," she said, "truth be told. But I am now."

"Me, too. So let's go do it. The whole world is out there waiting for us."

He jumped up, reached for her hand and pulled her to her feet.

"I can hardly wait," she said and fell into step beside him as they headed down the beach.

CHAPTER TWENTY-FOUR

One year later

LUCI GAZED OUT the window of the car she
and Cody had rented at Sea Tac airport. They
were driving through a forested area, but here
and there she caught glimpses of the wide-
open spaces that meant the ocean was nearby.
"Just a few more miles and we'll be there."

"Are you excited?" Cody slowed to nego-
tiate a turn in the winding road.

"Yes. Coming home is always exciting.
Don't you think?"

He shot her a smile. "All the more so this
time, because I'm with you."

So much had happened since that day
on the beach when she'd joyfully accepted
Cody's ring. First they'd flown to Denver to
meet Dex and Shar, who stood up with them
while they were married. Then they went to

LA to catch a flight to Peru and the archaeological expedition, where Luci was hired as a writer. Her job was to take the archaeologists' notes and write them up into formal reports, a task she found both challenging and interesting.

Now, they were taking a beach break, as Luci called it.

Finally the Welcome to Willow Beach sign came into view. Cody turned at Seaview Avenue, continued on a few blocks and then pulled into the driveway of his old home. Since Olive had married Mel and moved in with him, the house now belonged to Cody and Luci.

"I'm so glad to be home for a while," Luci said.

Cody put the car into Park and gazed at the house. "Me, too."

Surprised by his enthusiastic response, she said, "You mean that?"

"I do. I'm looking forward to sitting in my favorite chair, putting my feet up and vegging out in front of the TV. Guess I've become a nester, after all."

She laughed and kissed his cheek. "A part-time one, anyway."

They hauled in their bags, opened the windows and aired out the house. They hadn't been there long when Luci's mother phoned. "We're expecting you for dinner tonight," she said.

"We'll be there." Luci let a beat go by and then added, "How about the rest of the family?"

"Can't tell you any more. I want you to be surprised."

At the appointed time, Luci and Cody drove to the Monroe home. Cars and trucks were parked all along the driveway. Luci stared. "What's going on?"

Don stepped into view and waved them forward. Cody stopped and rolled down his window. "There's a spot saved for you over there." Don pointed to an empty space near the house.

Luci leaned across Cody and asked, "What's happening?"

Don's eyes twinkled. "You'll find out soon enough."

Cody parked the car and they got out. Holding hands, they walked around the side of the house. As they stepped into the backyard, someone shouted, "They're here!" and a cheer went up.

When she saw the banner proclaiming Welcome Home, Cody and Luci! she pressed her hand to her cheek. The backyard was filled with people. For the next few minutes, they were busy exchanging hugs and handshakes. The party included Olive and Mel; Ben and Sylvie; Glen Thomas and his wife; Marge Delano and her husband; Eva and Mark Townson; Tessa and Carl, and so many more that Luci lost count as she and Cody circulated among the guests.

"I'm gonna have to take some pictures." Cody was already reaching for his camera. "This is too good an opportunity to pass up."

"Go for it, honey," Luci said, having become quite accustomed to her husband's addiction to his profession and loving him all the more for it.

While Cody took his photos, Luci joined her father and mother, who stood together on the patio near the barbecue, where her father was keeping an eye on his chicken. "Mom, Dad, I'm so glad to be home again. Having us all together is like old times."

Her father put his arm around Luci's shoulders and gave her a hug. "Our family's complete now you're here."

"We've missed you," Anna said, kissing Luci's cheek. "And I'm looking forward to hearing all about your and Cody's adventures."

"And I want to hear about yours, too," Luci said. "Especially that cruise you two went on to celebrate your wedding anniversary."

"That was special," Anna said, smiling at Erv, who grinned back and grasped her hand.

When the food was ready, they all trooped to the buffet table. The salads included Olive's potato salad and the desserts Anna's sponge cake. After dinner, while Cody exchanged stories with Max Billings, Ben and Don, Francine and Luci wandered to Anna's rose garden, where the lowering sun highlighted the red, orange and yellow blossoms.

"So Dad and Mom are getting along now?" Luci asked.

Francine nodded. "Like they're on a honeymoon. They really do love each other."

Luci fingered one of the rose blossoms, the petals soft and moist to the touch. "What about you and Will?"

"I'm still living in Oceanside, but we're

going to counseling. And guess what? I'm a Girl Scout leader now."

"That's wonderful, Fran. I'm sure Betsy and Megan appreciate spending time with their mom."

As they continued their stroll, Luci spotted her father and brother drinking coffee together on the patio. "Looks like Don and Dad are speaking again."

"Oh, yes. Dad even went fishing on Don's new boat."

"Has Arliss accepted Don's new job?"

Francine tilted her head to the side, then said, "More or less. She loves her new day-care business, says it keeps her busy when he's gone."

"She does love kids," Luci said.

Jason ran up to them. "Auntie Luci, Auntie Fran, look at our airport." He pointed to a strip of sand at the edge of the yard where Spencer, Hannah, Betsy and Megan were playing with the toy airplanes. "We're going to get one that really flies," Jason said. "Grandpa promised."

"He did, did he?" Luci asked, ruffling his hair.

"He sure did. He's the best grandpa ever." Jason ran off to join the other children.

"I'm glad to see him being part of the family," Luci said as she and Francine headed back to the party.

"Yes, when Helen's in town, she always brings him over for a visit."

"She doesn't come, though?"

"No, but Mabel Thompson brought her to the garden club, and I'm told she and Mom talked to each other. Seems they both love roses. Not that they'd ever become best friends, but for Jason's sake, it's nice they're on speaking terms."

"I'm glad for that, too."

"What about you and Cody? Will you be in town long?"

"A couple months, at least. We have a lot to do here. Our first collaboration, a photo essay, is on exhibit at the Blue Gull Gallery. Then we've decided to do a book on the history of Willow Beach."

"That should keep you two busy," Fran commented.

They'd reached the patio, where Cody and Don joined them. "Did I hear my name mentioned?" Cody slipped his arm around Luci's shoulders.

"I was just telling Fran about all our projects," Luci said.

Don gave Cody a soft punch on his shoulder. "I told you that you two would make a good team."

"And you were right, buddy," Cody said. "You were right."

Later, after the party was over and everyone had gone home, Luci and Cody took a walk on the beach. Hand in hand, they strolled along, watching the moon rise and cast a silver glow over the water. "This is the best homecoming ever," she said.

"It is," he agreed. "Because we're together." He pulled her into his arms and gave her a kiss that left no doubt about the depth of his love.

Luci sighed with contentment. Her life wasn't perfect and never would be, but as long as she was with Cody, she'd be perfectly happy.

* * * * *

LARGER-PRINT BOOKS!

GET 2 FREE
LARGER-PRINT NOVELS
PLUS 2 FREE
MYSTERY GIFTS

Love Inspired®

Larger-print novels are now available...

LILP15

LARGER-PRINT BOOKS!

GET 2 FREE
LARGER-PRINT NOVELS
PLUS 2 FREE
MYSTERY GIFTS

Love Inspired®
SUSPENSE
RIVETING INSPIRATIONAL ROMANCE

Larger-print novels are now available...

YES! Please send me **The Montana Mavericks Collection** in Larger Print. This collection begins with 3 FREE books and 2 FREE gifts (gifts valued at approx. $20.00 retail) in the first shipment, along with the other first 4 books from the collection! If I do not cancel, I will receive 8 monthly shipments until I have the entire 51-book Montana Mavericks collection. I will receive 2 or 3 FREE books in each shipment and I will pay just $4.99 US/ $5.89 CDN for each of the other four books in each shipment, plus $2.99 for shipping and handling per shipment.*If I decide to keep the entire collection, I'll have paid for only 32 books, because 19 books are FREE! I understand that accepting the 3 free books and gifts places me under no obligation to buy anything. I can always return a shipment and cancel at any time. My free books and gifts are mine to keep no matter what I decide.

263 HCN 2404   463 HCN 2404

Name	(PLEASE PRINT)	
Address		Apt. #
City	State/Prov.	Zip/Postal Code

Signature (if under 18, a parent or guardian must sign)

Mail to the **Reader Service:**

IN U.S.A.: P.O. Box 1867, Buffalo, NY 14240-1867
IN CANADA: P.O. Box 609, Fort Erie, Ontario L2A 5X3

* Terms and prices subject to change without notice. Prices do not include applicable taxes. Sales tax applicable in N.Y. Canadian residents will be charged applicable taxes. This offer is limited to one order per household. All orders subject to approval. Credit or debit balances in a customer's account(s) may be offset by any other outstanding balance owed by or to the customer. Please allow 4 to 6 weeks for delivery. Offer available while quantities last. Offer not available to Quebec residents.

> **Your Privacy**—The Reader Service is committed to protecting your privacy. Our Privacy Policy is available online at www.ReaderService.com or upon request from the Reader Service.
>
> We make a portion of our mailing list available to reputable third parties that offer products we believe may interest you. If you prefer that we not exchange your name with third parties, or if you wish to clarify or modify your communication preferences, please visit us at www.ReaderService.com/consumerschoice or write to us at Reader Service Preference Service, P.O. Box 9062, Buffalo, NY 14269. Include your complete name and address.

LARGER-PRINT BOOKS!
GET 2 FREE LARGER-PRINT NOVELS PLUS
2 FREE GIFTS!

HARLEQUIN

super romance

More Story...More Romance

READERSERVICE.COM

Manage your account online!

- Review your order history
- Manage your payments
- Update your address

We've designed the Reader Service website just for you.

Enjoy all the features!

- Discover new series available to you, and read excerpts from any series.
- Respond to mailings and special monthly offers.
- Connect with favorite authors at the blog.
- Browse the Bonus Bucks catalog and online-only exculsives.
- Share your feedback.

Visit us at:

ReaderService.com